Talk Sweetly to Me

COURTNEY MILAN

This is a work of fiction. Names, characters, places, and incidents are the product of the author's imagination or are used fictitiously. Any resemblance to actual events, locales, or persons, living or dead, is purely coincidental.

Talk Sweetly to Me: © 2014 by Courtney Milan.
Cover design © Courtney Milan.

Cover photographs © Deborah Kolb | shutterstock.com.
Digital Edition 1.0

For Lucas, my partner in crime, clock-breaking, and quantum mechanics.

Chapter One

Greenwich, November 1882

THERE WAS NO WAY FOR Miss Rose Sweetly to set down her packages. All six of them were balanced precariously under one arm while her free hand fumbled through her pocket. Her fingers encountered used pencil nubs and a letter folded in half; her burdens shifted slightly, sliding away... If that dratted key ring was not in this pocket, and in the opposite instead—ah!

Thumb and forefinger met cold metal. Rose was withdrawing her find in triumph when a voice interrupted.

"Good afternoon, Miss Sweetly."

The sound of Mr. Shaughnessy's voice—that lilting velvet—set the inevitable in motion. First the book wrapped in paper slipped; then, as she grabbed for that, her notebook began to fall. She could compute the physics of it in her mind, a cascading avalanche of packages resulting from too few hands and too much gravity. Rose had time to make only one decision: save her slide rule or save the shopping?

Her slide rule won. She grabbed hold of the leather case with her fingertips just before it hit the ground.

Her other burdens were not so lucky. *Splat* went the book. The shopping landed with a more complex sound—one that smacked of breaking eggs. Three oranges escaped the bag entirely and bounced crazily down the pavement.

Mr. Stephen Shaughnessy stood two doors down from her. His eyebrows rose at this minor catastrophe, and Rose felt her cheeks heat. But there was nothing to do now but brazen it out.

She gave him her most brilliant smile and waved her slide rule case. "Good afternoon, Mr. Shaughnessy."

The case slipped slightly, but she managed to catch it before an even greater disaster ensued.

Mr. Shaughnessy had taken the house just down from her sister's three months ago. In all that time, she'd never managed to shake the nerves she felt around him. He had never done anything to warrant that nervousness, unfortunately; he was unfailingly polite.

As proof, he didn't abuse her for her clumsiness now. He didn't even remark on it. He simply came toward her. He took three steps forward—and she drew back one—before she realized that he only intended to pick up her oranges.

Any other reason he might have drawn close to her? That was all in her imagination.

She set down her slide rule carefully and picked up her shopping bag. It was canvas, and most of the contents hadn't spilled. The meat, wrapped in waxed paper, was still at the bottom. The eggs…well, she'd check them once they were inside, but she had a sneaking suspicion that she and her sister would be having omelets for dinner tonight. Only the fruit had truly gone awry. She picked up an apple, not looking in his direction.

But she didn't have to look directly at him to be aware of him. Mr. Shaughnessy was a young man—scarcely a few years older than she. He was tall and built on lovely, well-muscled lines, the sort that young ladies who intended to stay innocent were not supposed to notice. He had a friendly smile, one that made a woman want to smile in response, and the faintest hint of an Irish accent. He had dark hair, dark eyes, and a much darker reputation.

But he picked up one of the offending fruits and smiled in her direction. "Why is it that the oranges bounced, but the apples did not?"

His smile felt like an arrow, one that struck her straight in the solar plexus. And so Rose adjusted her spectacles on her nose and said the first thing that came to mind.

Unfortunately, the first thing that came to mind was…

"It's Newton's Third Law. Upon collision, the apple exerts a force on the pavement, and so the pavement must exert an equal and opposite force on the apple. The structure of the apple is inelastic and so the apple bruises. The orange, by contrast…" She swallowed, realized that she was babbling, and shut her mouth. "I'm sorry, Mr. Shaughnessy. I don't think that's what you meant to ask, was it?"

He straightened. Oh, he was dreadfully handsome. He put a casual care into his appearance, and it showed. He was clean-shaven, even though it was three in the afternoon. His cravat looked as crisp as if it had been pressed just now, not at six in the morning. Nothing about Mr. Shaughnessy suggested that he was a degenerate of the first order. Nothing, that was, except his line of work and the persistent gossip in the papers.

"You don't need to let me natter on when I get distracted that way," she told him. "Everyone else stops me. In these parts, it's considered polite to interrupt Miss Sweetly when she's on a tear."

"Nonsense," Mr. Shaughnessy said. He took a step toward her, and then another. Her chest constricted—he was standing so dreadfully, deliciously close—and then he held out the oranges he'd gathered.

For one moment, as she took them from him, their hands brushed. Neither of them was wearing gloves: she, because she couldn't have found her keys while wearing them; he because…well, the heavens alone knew, and she was not about to ask. His fingers were warm and pale against hers.

"I would never interrupt you," he told her. "I love it when you talk Sweetly to me."

She yanked her hand away. "You mustn't say things like that, Mr. Shaughnessy. Someone might overhear and mistake your meaning."

His eyes met hers. For the briefest second, she imagined a spark in them—as if some imp inside him whispered that anyone who heard what he'd said would understand it perfectly. He'd intended to flirt, and he knew precisely how he'd flustered her.

But he didn't say that. He simply shrugged. "We wouldn't want anyone to misunderstand."

If there had been an ounce of sarcasm in his voice, she would have walked away right then and there. But there wasn't.

"So let me say it better. If I didn't want to hear you talk about your opposite and equal reactions, I wouldn't ask about your star charts. What are you computing this time?"

"Oh, it's not star charts, not today. It won't be star charts for months. It's the Great Comet now, and it'll be the transit of Venus after that."

His eyebrows rose. "There's a great comet?"

"Do you not read any scientific papers? It may be the brightest comet ever observed. You can still see it with the naked eye against the sun itself."

He glanced upward at the sun overhead, unobscured by any cometary tail. "If you can see it with the naked eye, how is it that I've never caught a glimpse of it?"

She huffed. "Because London is not in the southern hemisphere. The visibility here is not as it is in Melbourne, for instance."

"Ah."

"In any event, Finlay in Cape Town wired his measurements to Dr. Barnstable, and he's set me to do the computing."

"So what does it look like?"

She got out her notebook, opened it to the appropriate page.

"Here we are. The comet transited the sun a little more than a month ago."

He stared for a moment at the column of numbers she was pointing to, and then gave his head a shake. "Right."

She felt herself flush again. But before she could manage to work up a good case of embarrassment, he had interrupted her, pointing to an orange in her bag.

"So let's say that is the sun. Then where is the comet?"

"Don't be ridiculous, Mr. Shaughnessy. If that orange represents the sun, we here on Earth would be standing seventy-one feet away."

"Seventy-one?" he asked mildly.

"Seventy-one point five eight three, by the last measure of the distance between the earth and the sun, but I try not to be pedantic. It makes people laugh at me." Rose pointed to a dot on her notebook page. "Imagine that *this* is the sun. Then we are a speck of unimaginable smallness here." She indicated a spot some inches away. "The comet, then, traveled along this path…" Her finger, dark against the white page, etched an elliptical curve. "But that's not the exciting part. You see, anyone can calculate the path of a comet given enough data."

"Not anyone," he murmured.

She waved this away. "From all accounts, the nucleus of this comet split sometime after perihelion. Dr. Barnstable believes that we can predict the path of each piece—and since they're so close to each other now, it will be no simple matter. It's a three-body problem, which means it's impossible to solve with equations. He's asked me to work it out for him." She beamed up at him.

He smiled back. "That's brilliant, Miss Sweetly."

"Of course," she started to explain, "we'll be wrong, but it's *how* we're wrong that is most exciting. You see—"

The door opened behind them. Rose jumped again. This time, she managed to keep hold of her shopping bag. She turned to see her sister standing in the doorway. Patricia had one hand on the door handle; the other was placed in the small of her back. She was wearing a voluminous pink gown and a matching kerchief covering her hair. Her eyebrows rose at the scene in front of her, but her dark eyes sparkled in amusement.

"And here I thought I heard you at the door ages ago," Patricia said. She gave her a head an exasperated shake, but Rose was certain—mostly certain—that she smiled as she did it. Patricia stooped as best as she could. Her heavy belly made her awkward, but she plucked Rose's key off the ground. "Ah. I see that I did."

"I...dropped some things," Rose said, flushing all over again. "I was picking them up."

Patricia looked at Rose's notebook, open in her hands. She looked at Mr. Shaughnessy, standing not two feet away. And then she glanced at the pavement, where Rose's other packages—the mail, the paper, the wrapped-up book—still lay scattered. "Yes," she said dryly. "I can see that. That explains everything."

"I'll let you go, then," Mr. Shaughnessy said. He tipped his hat. "Miss Sweetly. Mrs. Wells."

"Mr. Shaughnessy." Rose nodded her head. "I would curtsey, but the apples cannot withstand another inelastic collision."

Beside her, Patricia made a noise in protest. But she held out her hands, gesturing. Rose gave her the book and her slide rule case. While Mr. Shaughnessy disappeared around the corner of the street, she picked up the last of her scattered things.

Patricia did not berate her immediately. She did not, in fact, berate her at all. She would normally have offered to help Rose, but she was eight months pregnant, ungainly and awkward, and bending over did not come easily to her. When they'd gathered everything, they retreated inside the house—Rose at a walk, Patricia at a waddle.

Patricia did not say anything as they traversed the front drawing room and went into the back pantry. She didn't speak until Rose had the shopping spread out in front of them.

"Rose," Patricia said quietly, "have you considered going back to Papa?"

Rose had not. Her stomach clenched at the very thought. "How could I leave you, when Dr. Wells will not return from his tour of duty for more than a week yet? I *promised* him."

Patricia's husband was a naval physician. He'd bent sent to Sierra Leone around the time Patricia had realized she was with child, and Rose had come to attend her sister in his absence. But it wasn't just her sister's welfare that had Rose worried. Their parents lived in London—so close, and yet impossibly far from the Royal Observatory. At her father's house, there would be no computations, no comets.

No Mr. Shaughnessy to set her nerves on edge.

"You know," Patricia said, "you *know* that he is the most incredible rake." She did not say who *he* was. She didn't need to.

Rose set the oranges in a bowl, refusing to look at her sister. "He's never once offered to seduce me. I don't even think he's thought of it."

"He's thought of it," Patricia said dryly. "And frankly, Rose, the way he's talking to you? I don't think he'll even need to offer."

Rose let out a long breath and shut her eyes. It was, unfortunately, true. Mr. Shaughnessy was…well, he just *was*. His name had been on all the ladies' lips since Rose was seventeen, when he'd earned renown—or infamy, depending on who was speaking—as the first man to write a column of advice for the *Women's Free Press*, a radical paper that Rose should not have enjoyed nearly as much as she did. In the five years since his first column, he'd only built upon that reputation. He'd published four novels. His books were called "masterpieces of satire" by some, and "dangerous rubbish that was best burned unread" by others.

They had, by all accounts, sold well—and those who harrumphed about setting bonfires with them were the ones most likely to furtively purchase them in brown paper packaging.

Mooning after Mr. Stephen Shaughnessy was foolish. She knew how they looked, sketched to scale. Socially speaking, if he were an orange in Westminster, she was…an elderberry, somewhere in the vicinity of Tanzania.

"I love you, Rose." Patricia sighed. "And I know you'll make a good marriage, one as brilliant as mine. But you have to remember that most of the men who look at you won't be seeing *you*. They won't see that you're clever and amusing." Her sister came forward and took Rose's hand in her own. "They'll see *this*." She rubbed the back of Rose's hand. Dark skin pressed against dark skin. "It doesn't matter how respectably you dress or how much you insist. Most men will see only that you're black and they'll think you're available. So please take care, Rose. I don't wish you hurt."

Rose polished the last apple with a towel. "Don't worry about that," she said softly. "I won't do anything foolish."

She didn't say anything about getting hurt. There was no point worrying about that. She thought of Mr. Shaughnessy's smile, of the wicked gleam in his eye. She thought of him asking her about oranges and comets, of him looking at her and saying in that dark, dangerous, lilting tone *I love it when you talk Sweetly to me.*

She'd also seen the notes about him in the gossip columns. He was utterly outrageous, and no matter how he made her feel, the last thing she needed was an outrageous man.

No, there was no point worrying about getting hurt.

At this point, pain was already inevitable.

Chapter Two

OF ALL THE WAYS that Stephen Shaughnessy had ever decided to torment himself, this one had to be the most diabolical.

There was a slight musty smell to the offices a few streets from the Royal Observatory, as if the windows were not often opened. The books on the shelves around him ranged from an ancient set of Newton's *Philosophiae Naturalis Principia Mathematica* to a report on something called spectroscopic observations; the walls were a yellowing whitewash over which charts had been tacked year after year, until only a few spots remained bare.

The room was, in short, little better than a dingy pit, the only decorations a celebration of mathematics—a subject he had never excelled at, and, until recently, had never found interesting.

Which was precisely what made his next sentence so shocking.

"Yes," he heard himself saying aloud. "It is a real pleasure to meet you, Dr. Barnstable. I'm terribly impressed by your work."

Even more shockingly, the statement was true.

"No, no. The pleasure is assuredly all mine." Dr. Barnstable caught Stephen's hand in his and gave it a few enthusiastic pumps. "I cannot believe you've heard of me—and that you follow astronomy." He smiled bemusedly. "Truly, I feel dazed by the prospect."

He could hardly feel as dazed as Stephen himself. It had taken him almost a month to realize what was happening and another four weeks to succumb to utter madness. Or mathematics; he wasn't sure there was any distinction at this point.

Dr. Barnstable was an older man in his sixties, with six inches of white beard as proof of his age. But there was nothing fusty about him; he shook Stephen's hand with a firm grip.

"Your paper on the orbit of double stars is a true classic," Stephen said.

The point when Stephen had read it, searching for any hints of Miss Sweetly's contribution to the piece, was the point when he'd known that it was over. It had been like a newspaper headline printed in two-inch type: *There's no use struggling, Stephen. You're well and truly caught.*

"My wife is an absolute enthusiast of your work." Barnstable's eyes sparkled. "She reads me pointed bits from your column. I ought to take you to task—giving away all our masculine secrets—but ah, well." That last was delivered with an amused shake of his head.

"They're not secrets," Stephen explained. "Women already know everything I say. The only reason anything I say is amusing is because a man is saying it."

"Ha!" Barnstable jabbed Stephen's shoulder in a friendly fashion. "You're just as clever in person as you are on paper. Well. I can't say I disagree. Times are surely changing, and for the better. You have no idea how much easier some of those recent advances have made my work."

Stephen actually had every idea. One of those "advances," he suspected, was Miss Rose Sweetly—and from what little he could tell, she'd done very well for Barnstable indeed. The man had better praise her.

"But never mind that," Barnstable said. "We can talk politics some other time. What can I do for you?"

"I'm doing research on astronomy," he said.

"For your next novel? Are you writing about an astronomer, by chance?"

Stephen considered this and decided it was as good an explanation as any other he could offer. "Yes."

He'd made something of a career of speaking outrageous truths, but there was a time and a place for outraging people. Even he knew better than to admit what was really going on. *No, I'm just fascinated with a woman, and I want to know everything about her* would not go over well.

Barnstable nodded thoughtfully. "What would you like to know?"

"Oh dear." Stephen sighed. "I've tried to swot up on my own with woeful results. I need help with every detail, starting from how to calculate astronomical distances by parallax, on up through Kepler and the theory of planetary motion."

Barnstable blinked. "That is…quite a lot."

"Oh, I don't expect you to instruct me yourself. I'm sure you're too busy for that. I had imagined you would fob me off on someone else," Stephen said. "An assistant or a student—someone who wouldn't mind a little extra income."

"Ah." The man's expression cleared momentarily, but then he shook his head and frowned. "Hmm. My student is in the Bermudas at the moment—he's observing the transit of Venus, lucky boy. Were it not for my knee…" Barnstable trailed off, shaking his head. "That leaves only my computer. And…" He hesitated delicately. "She's a woman."

"Your computer?" Stephen asked with studied nonchalance. This was what he'd hoped for, after all. "What's that?"

"Precisely what it sounds like: a person who computes. Absolutely necessary for those of us engaged in any sort of dynamics. All those calculations come to a dreadful mess; if I had to do them all myself, I'd have no time to think of anything. And yes, my computer is a woman." He cleared his throat. "A woman of African descent. Those of my colleagues who are prejudiced on that score only deprive themselves of Miss Sweetly's assistance."

"Surely you don't think I would share their prejudices," Stephen said. "Your wife has been making you read my work, yes?"

Barnstable's smile became pained. "It isn't that. Or it isn't only that. You see, she's a woman. And you…"

"Oh." Stephen smiled. "That. I suppose I do have something of a reputation."

It was hard-earned, that reputation. Occasionally inconvenient, but it was what it was.

"Yes," Barnstable said apologetically. "That. And Miss Sweetly is, alas, a very young woman. She's not quite of age yet. I've an arrangement with her father—my wife must be with her at all times in the building. He'd not like to see anything happen to her, and quite selfishly, I'd not like to lose her, either. She would be ideal if only she were a man. But…"

Stephen wouldn't be here if she were a man. He still couldn't quite believe he'd come.

"Maybe she could manage a lesson or three? Just something to get me started until your student returns. Your wife might stay in the room with us, of course, to avoid any impropriety."

"I don't know…" Dr. Barnstable rubbed at his beard.

"Ask her what she thinks," Stephen suggested. "After all, 'not quite of age' for women often means we'd send younger men into battle. Or to the Bermudas to watch the transit of Venus."

Barnstable nodded thoughtfully at that.

"And I do have a reputation. I won't pretend I haven't earned it. But I've never seduced an innocent before. In truth, I do more acquiescing than I do seducing. So unless you fear that your computer will seduce *me*…"

Barnstable snorted. "Well. I suppose a few hours with her, with my wife present, could not hurt. If she agrees, that is."

The older man left, and Stephen paced to the window. From here, he could see bare tree branches and grass, once a brilliant green, now fading to a less vibrant color.

He really wasn't sure what he was about. He *wasn't* planning to seduce her, not really. It would be a terrible thing for a man like him to do to a woman in Miss Sweetly's position, and he had a very firm rule that he did not do terrible things to people in general, and to women in particular. Liking a woman—even liking her very well—was more reason to adhere to the rule, not less.

As far as he could tell, he *was* just tormenting himself.

A noise sounded in the hall; he caught the low murmur of voices, and then the office door scraped open. Stephen turned from the window to face the newcomers.

Barnstable stood in the doorway. Behind him were two figures. The first was a heavy silhouette of an older woman with a substantial bustle; the second figure, far more familiar, hid herself behind the other woman's bulk. She was scarcely visible in the dim hall light. Still, Stephen felt his pulse begin to accelerate.

He stood and addressed himself to the first woman. "You must be Mrs. Barnstable."

"Mr. Shaughnessy, this is my wife, Mrs. Barnstable." Dr. Barnstable stepped to one side.

The woman behind him moved into the room, all smiles. "Oh, Mr. Shaughnessy! It is such a pleasure to meet you. After all these years of reading your words! I adore—absolutely adore—everything that you write."

"Of course you adore what I write," he said. "You must be a woman of excellent taste. I'm delighted to make your acquaintance."

"I shall have palpitations of the heart," Mrs. Barnstable announced. "Listen to me, going on like a green girl. I sound like a chicken, squawking away. What must you think of me? I'm not silly. I'm not. It's just that I've been reading your work for years now. Can you..." Her lashes fluttered down. "Can you do the *Actual Man* thing?"

The advice column he wrote was entitled "Ask a Man"—and women wrote to him in droves to do just that. He signed every column almost precisely the same way.

"If you'd like." Stephen looked into Mrs. Barnstable's face.

The woman's eyes grew wide; a hand drifted up to touch her throat as if to touch nonexistent pearls. He let his voice drop down a few notes and imbued his next words with all the wicked intent that he could muster.

"I'm Stephen Shaughnessy," he said. "Actual Man."

Mrs. Barnstable let out a wavering sigh. "Are you as wicked as the gossip papers say, young man?"

He didn't *feel* wicked. "Oh, no," he said, lowering one eyelid in a lazy wink. "The papers don't know the half of it."

"If you're that bad, then I mustn't introduce you to my charge."

In direct contradiction to these brave words, Mrs. Barnstable turned around. She took Miss Sweetly by the elbow, drawing her into the room. "Miss Sweetly, look who it is! It's Stephen Shaughnessy—and I know how you delight in his column."

That was not a proper introduction. It wasn't even an *improper* introduction. It left Miss Sweetly at a horrendous disadvantage, after all, putting her directly into the class of enthusiasts like Mrs. Barnstable.

Miss Sweetly was many things, but effusive she was not. She dropped him a little curtsey. "I do read your column, Mr. Shaughnessy." Her voice was quiet and subdued in comparison with Mrs. Barnstable's.

When she looked up at him, though, she seemed anything but subdued. Her dark hair, just a little frizzy, had been tamed and wrestled into a bun. She wore a demure gown—not one of the fashionable creations that a lady might wear, but a sensible, high-necked muslin, a thing of long sleeves and buttons that his fingers itched to undo. The fabric hinted at curves of breast and hip; her bustle, less pronounced, could not quite hide her figure.

Her eyes were dark and still, and he felt as if he'd been struck over the head—as if he were looking up into a night sky, bright with stars.

He gave her a little bow. "Miss Sweetly."

"Oh, yes," Mrs. Barnstable said, shaking her head as if she had just now remembered her duty. "Mr. Shaughnessy, this is Miss Rose Sweetly, Dr. Barnstable's computer. She is very young, although I suppose to a thing like you, she'd not seem so. But she's ever so clever."

"I'm always happy to meet clever young ladies," Stephen said. "They're my second favorite kind."

Miss Sweetly grimaced at this in embarrassment and lifted a hand to adjust her spectacles.

She had no idea what that simple motion did to Stephen. It made him want to do the same himself—to run his fingers up the line of her nose, slowly tracing that elegant curve. To hook his finger under the bridge of her glasses and slide them down her face, and then…

But Miss Sweetly did not ask about his favorite kind of young lady, and the answer that he'd come up with to that obvious question went to waste. Over the months of their acquaintance, she'd always forced him to deviate from his usual responses. When he was around her, he had to think, to pay attention—because she never said what he expected.

She did not mention that she knew him. She did not, in fact, say anything at all. She simply looked over Mrs. Barnstable's shoulder, out the window, as if she had more important things than Stephen Shaughnessy on her mind.

It had always been like that with her. The first day he'd met her, he had run into her on the street—quite literally, as they had both been distracted, and neither of them had been watching where they were going. He'd asked what had her so deep in thought, and she had told him.

It had been the most intense experience of his life, seeing her transform from a shy, nervous miss into a magician who intended to coax secrets from the sky. He'd never found mathematics erotic before that day, but watching her lips form the words "parabola" and "Newtonian step" had been utterly riveting. He had been riveted ever since.

"Mr. Shaughnessy wants someone to show him around a slide rule," Mrs. Barnstable was saying to Rose. "And teach him a few tricks. It's for his next book. And he's even offered to pay—what was that again, Mr. Shaughnessy? Three shillings per lesson? Is that what you said? Isn't that generous!"

He hadn't said anything of the sort, but he had to smile at the effrontery of the woman. Three shillings per lesson was downright exorbitant.

"Of course," Mrs. Barnstable said, "most of that fee will go to you, Miss Sweetly, but as I will have to chaperone, I'll expect sixpence per lesson, and another sixpence for my help in the negotiations."

No, Mrs. Barnstable was not the fluttery mother hen she made herself out to be. But right now, it was not Mrs. Barnstable's approval or her heart, mercenary though it might be, that he cared about. It was Miss Sweetly's.

"Are you going to do the *Actual Man* thing to me, too?" she asked, not looking up at him.

"No," he said with a shake of his head. "You sound apprehensive about it, and I try to do that only where it's appreciated."

She sniffed.

"Don't look so disbelieving, Miss Sweetly. I'm a simple man. I like being appreciated."

"At three shillings a lesson," Mrs. Barnstable put in, "you could appreciate him a little."

Miss Sweetly shut her eyes.

"Oh, dear." Mrs. Barnstable said. "That did come out rather unfortunately. I didn't intend…"

But she couldn't even say what she hadn't intended. Normally, watching others struggle with the ridiculous strictures of propriety was one of Stephen's favorite pastimes. He usually waited until all the feathers were smoothed and everyone was on the verge of sighing in relief. Then he'd come out with something utterly inappropriate—blasting all the careful wordings and euphemisms to bits with a brazen determination.

Now, however, he held his tongue. It was an unfamiliar skill, as rarely used and as poorly understood as his mathematics.

"You don't have to appreciate me," he said to Miss Sweetly. "Just teach me to use a slide rule and explain a few basics, and I'll appreciate you."

She looked over at him. For a long while, she seemed to contemplate this. Finally, she nodded. "I suppose I might. If Dr. Barnstable would not mind."

Permission being granted all around, she escorted him to a smaller office, one that was even dingier than the last, which he hadn't thought possible. A typewriter sat at one desk; Mrs. Barnstable sat behind it, fussing about her piles of paper, before settling on one and picking it up.

Miss Sweetly's familiar portfolio graced the other desk; she gestured him to a chair next to hers. He sat.

"Miss Sweetly," he whispered in a low voice, "I know I've rather trapped you into this, but if you'd prefer I leave, that I not bother you, you've only to say the word."

She looked up at him. "But we speak on the streets all the time. Is this so different?"

It was not so different; it was simply an escalation.

"If you wish for a more robust chaperone than Mrs. Barnstable, I'm happy to find someone else." He met her eyes, holding her gaze for a long, fraught moment, before adding, "Only if you wish it, of course."

She raised an eyebrow and glanced behind them. "Mrs. Barnstable," she told him in a low voice, "falls asleep at her desk in the afternoons. She means well, but she *is* sixty-three."

"Oh, no." He leaned forward and pitched his voice even lower. "How dreadfully unchaperoned that will leave us."

She pursed her lips. "The door is open. Chaperones are for ladies; I'm a shopkeeper's daughter. So long as I have recourse if you forget yourself, whatever could happen?"

"Whatever indeed?"

She had looked back at him as he spoke; now she was looking into his eyes, swaying in place a little, almost mesmerized. He felt the slightest twinge of conscience.

He didn't *intend* to seduce her. But he expected he could; it wouldn't prove too difficult. But he didn't want this to end with her guilt and self-recrimination. In point of fact, he didn't want this to end at all.

"If you're going to write a book that touches on astronomy, we had better teach you the basics. Let's start you off with multiplication." Her voice, when she finally spoke, was a little squeaky.

"Naturally," Stephen said, pitching his voice too low for Mrs. Barnstable to hear. "It's a Biblical command, after all: Be fruitful and multiply."

She did not look terribly impressed by that. Instead, she undid the metal fastenings of her slide rule case and took out the instrument.

"I should let you know," he went on, "I've managed to avoid being fruitful thus far. But I *do* enjoy a good session of multiplication."

She swallowed. "Mr. Shaughnessy," she said reproachfully, glancing over at Mrs. Barnstable.

But the older woman just smiled at them, oblivious to the improper turn of the conversation.

"Ah, was that too much?" he asked. "I can hold myself back, if I must."

She looked down at her hands. They were poised over her slide rule, her skin contrasting with the pale, graduated celluloid of the instrument. "Hold yourself back from the Bible, Mr. Shaughnessy?" She smiled faintly. "Why would I want you to do that? I imagine you need all the godliness you can muster."

"I imagine I do. Let's multiply, then."

She gave him another level look. But instead of reproaching him, she moved the slide rule between them, caressing it with a light touch.

"This is the slide." Her long, slender fingers demonstrated, moving the middle bar in a motion that he could not help but find analogous to another act. The thought of her fingers touching him in that slow, steady manner sent his mind whirling down another path altogether, one that left him feeling uncomfortably aroused.

"The left index," she said. "The right index. This metal window is called the cursor."

He nodded and tried to think of mathematics.

"So to multiply two numbers—let us say three and two—you move the left index to the three and set the cursor on the two." She demonstrated, her fingers working with a swift, practiced precision. "Then you can read the answer from the bottom scale."

He looked down. "Six," he said.

"Excellent." Her tone was almost brisk and business-like—almost, but for that slight hint of a quaver in it. "Now I shall write out a few problems. I expect you to calculate them using the slide rule."

She took out a piece of paper and began writing numbers down the side—lots of numbers, as if he were a child tasked with working problems. She wrote swiftly, in a clear, defined hand and slid the page over to him.

He knew he had an effect on her—the same effect he had on most women. He could dazzle her temporarily. But she did not stay dazzled, and he was not used to being so flummoxed in response.

"Let me know when you're finished," she said.

He looked at the paper. "You're not going to multiply with me?"

"No," she said somewhat severely. "You're going to multiply on your own. But I'll make you a wager. If I can finish my calculation of the projected cometary trajectory without the use of my slide rule before you can multiply a few piddling two-digit numbers…"

He took the paper from her. "What will I win, then?"

"Another lesson on multiplication."

He laughed softly. "And if I don't?"

"Then we'll head straight to division," she said briskly.

So saying, she opened her portfolio. He saw a bewildering column of numbers—interspersed with a few Greek deltas and epsilons—before she bent her head over them.

He'd heard her talk about her work. She'd occasionally done complicated long division in her head as she explained something to him on the streets. He'd known she was a genius—she spilled genius all around her without even having to think of it. But watching her work was one of the most astonishing things he had ever witnessed.

The paper was divided into five columns, each carefully labeled. She had to have been multiplying nine-digit numbers in her head without a moment's hesitation, marking them down on the paper as swiftly as she could write. He vaguely recognized something that he thought might have been the gravitational constant, if only his woeful knowledge of dimly recalled physics meant something…

"You're not multiplying," she said severely. But she didn't look at him. Instead, she adjusted her spectacles on her nose.

"Miss Sweetly, why on earth do you even have a slide rule?" he asked in amazement.

She still didn't look up. "There are trigonometric functions on the reverse of the slide. And occasionally, I need it as an aid to correct someone who believes I might be wrong." She frowned. "Mostly, though, I find it comforting."

He shook his head and started on his multiplication.

She did not finish before him—even though she'd filled four pages of calculations and had marked a cometary path about ten degrees further along. It was obvious that she had not intended to finish before him. She'd made that little wager as a sop to his pride. Boasting that he had finished first would have been like a child sketching a line drawing of a man, and then crowing that it had taken less time than it had taken Michelangelo to complete the Sistine Chapel.

He sat and watched her figure instead.

He knew Miss Sweetly was charmed by him. She was too nervous in his company not to be. When they talked, she winced as she spoke, sometimes shaking her head as if to contradict her own words. It was only when she talked mathematics that he could see this side of her—sure and steady, swift and beautiful, as if when she was surrounded by numbers, she forgot that she was supposed to be shy.

Behind them, he could hear Mrs. Barnstable snoring. Precisely as Miss Sweetly had predicted.

She looked up after a moment and noticed that he was done. She glanced over his paper with a practiced eye.

"That proved easy enough," she said.

"What is next, Miss Sweetly? You did promise me more multiplication."

She nodded. She had lost that air of uncertainty; she was in her mathematical element now, and it showed.

"Let us calculate a very small number," she said. "How about a probability? Do you know much of probabilities?"

"A little." He made a motion with his hand.

"Well, then. I'll make this one simple. What do you suppose the chances are that I will be foolish?"

He looked over at her. "Shy?" he asked. "Or stupid?"

She winced a little at that, but didn't look away. "The latter, if you please."

"Then I'd put it at no better than one in a thousand."

"Very well, then. Multiply that by the possibility of our meeting while alone—let us call that one in four—and that by the chance that you will be charming."

His interest was piqued now. He had no idea what she was computing, but he'd be happy to find her alone and charm her into whatever number she wished. He leaned forward. "Tell me. What *is* the chance that you'll find me charming?"

"I'd approximate it as…" She looked across the room thoughtfully, her finger tapping against her lips. "I suppose I should be generous; you are paying for these lessons. So let us say forty percent."

"A mere forty percent?" Stephen clutched his chest dramatically. "A knife to the heart! You slay me, Miss Sweetly."

Her finger did not stop tapping, but she smiled as shyly as if he'd offered her a compliment. "You misidentify the weapon. It's not a knife."

"No?"

Miss Sweetly shook her head. "It's a double slide rule from Elliots, and I have found it extremely useful in dispatching all manner of men. Especially the ones given to excess histrionics. Now shall we continue the calculation?"

He sat back, smiling faintly. "By all means. I can see where this is heading. I have always wanted to be abused with numbers."

She huffed. "The chance that my father would not discover the whole thing before it proved too late is one in ten, and the possibility that I should be hit on the head with an anvil, or a similarly heavy item, is perhaps one in a million. Tell me, Mr. Shaughnessy, what is the probability of all those things occurring in conjunction?"

"Ah…" He had to use paper to keep track. "That would be…a chance of one in…a hundred billion?"

"Ooh." She winced. "That's a very small number. I'm exceedingly sorry for you, Mr. Shaughnessy."

"It is." He looked at the figure. "What, precisely, was I calculating?"

She looked up at him. For one moment, he thought she was going to be shy again—that she would move away and shake her head rather than answer. But even though her voice was low, she still said the words.

"That," she told him, "is the chance that you'll be able to seduce me."

His mouth went dry, and he coughed heavily. "A slide rule to the heart," he heard himself say. "Ouch. Is that what you think of me? That I'm trying to get you alone so that I can seduce you?"

She met his eyes. "What else am I supposed to think when you show up at my place of work, pretend not to know me, and inveigle lessons with me from my employer? What else would you be trying to do, Mr. Shaughnessy?"

He blinked. He opened his mouth and then very slowly closed it again.

"I don't know."

She scoffed.

"I don't know," he repeated. "But coming here, lying to Dr. Barnstable, lying to you just to seduce you—that sounds like a sinister plot. I don't have sinister plots, Miss Sweetly; they take too much work. I'm here because I would like to spend more time with you, and because I love listening to you talk about mathematics. Nothing more villainous than that."

She clearly didn't believe him. Her nostrils flared ever so slightly; she turned away, setting her hand between them.

"Speaking of mathematics," he said, "why did an anvil appear in the midst of that calculation? I've done a great many things and even I have never had call to use an anvil."

She looked up into his eyes. "How else was I to acquire amnesia?" she asked shyly.

He blinked in confusion, then burst into laughter as he realized what she meant.

She frowned. "I'm not attempting to amuse you. I would need to forget not only my own moral sense, but my work, my family, my future—everything I would give up if you succeeded in such an aim."

"In that case," he promised, "let me set your mind at ease. I hereby adopt a strict no-anvil policy. If I ever have you in my bed, I want you to remember yourself. I like you. There's no point having your body if you're not included."

She should have smacked him for that, or at the very least, ordered him away. Instead, she touched her slide rule, moving the metal cursor back and forth.

"Then there's no point at all," she whispered.

Behind them, Mrs. Barnstable gave a snort. They both jumped, but the older woman only turned her head from side to side before subsiding once more.

"Haven't you been listening?" he asked in a low voice. "This—talking to you, just like this—is already the point. I like you. I like talking to you. If you don't like me, send me off."

She raised an eyebrow at him. And then, without answering, she began to write another set of numbers on a sheet of paper.

"Let's practice division," she said.

Anyone who heard her patient explanation might have thought her cool and earnest. Stephen knew better. She *hadn't* sent him off, and no matter what she was saying, the message was clear. She liked him—unwillingly, perhaps—but she still liked him.

He waited until he'd started on the problems she'd set for him, until she had picked up her pen and restarted her own calculations, before he spoke again.

"I have another question about that last probability."

She set down her pen. "Go ahead."

"You are always very exacting about the numbers you use. When you said I was forty percent likely to be charming…"

She blinked up at him. "I haven't done an accurate calculation, but yes. About forty percent. If you wish, I could collate—"

He shook his head. "I don't need a list. It's just to satisfy my own curiosity. Why only forty percent?"

She looked down. "My personal tastes—nothing you should worry over, really—"

"If I have not made it clear, Miss Sweetly, I take an avid interest in your personal tastes."

She let out a long breath. "I don't trust you," she said simply. "If you had half a chance, you'd take me to bed."

He could have denied it. But truthfully? He wasn't trying to shove her in that direction, but would he say no? Of course he wouldn't.

"Ah." He picked up the next sheet of problems she'd written out for him, found the next number on the slide. "Then you have nothing to worry about, not according to your calculations. You could find me charming all the time, and according to you, I'd still only have a chance of...of..." He fumbled.

She took pity on him. "One in forty billion."

"There, you see? I don't have half a chance. I'm not even within spitting range of a hundredth of a chance. So there can be no harm in your allowing yourself to be charmed by me all the time." So saying, he gave her a brilliant smile.

It affected her. It obviously affected her. Her hands tangled in her lap; she glanced down, not in demure deflection, but as if to avert her eyes from the sun. She rubbed the bridge of her nose, as if her spectacles chafed.

"You're trying to charm me with mathematics," she said.

"Is it working?"

She looked up at him. *Yes,* said her dark eyes, shining at him. *Yes,* said the part of her lips, the fingers that drew up to brush her hair. *Yes,* said the tilt of her body in his direction.

"No," she told him with a firm shake of her head. "It isn't."

Chapter Three

THAT NIGHT, ROSE DREAMED that a column of numbers was chasing her through some odd, non-Cartesian landscape, a vista of lines and swirling colors. In the distance, someone was laughing—not a cruel laugh, or even a laugh at her expense. Just a friendly, welcoming laugh.

The numbers caught her, taking hold of her shoulder. She jerked away, but they held her fast.

How did numbers *grip?* She turned to them, fascinated…and very groggily came awake.

The room was dark; the only illumination was a pale stripe of moonlight, filtered through an inch-wide gap in her curtains. No sound rose from the street; it was the dead of night indeed.

But there was a hand, warm, on Rose's shoulder. It gave her a little shake.

"Rose," Patricia whispered, "are you awake?"

"Patricia?" Rose turned to find her sister sitting on the bed next to her, her form dim in the night.

"It's started." Her sister's voice crackled with excitement, but the hand on Rose seemed tense, almost fearful.

Rose didn't need to ask what *it* was. There was only one *it* in the household these days.

She sat bolt upright in her bed. "What? Already? It's too soon."

"Thirty-six weeks, by Doctor Chillingsworth's count. It *is* too early—but I felt a most definite contraction. It's starting."

"It can't start. Isaac is—"

She cut herself off. Her sister's husband was not yet home. They'd been so sure he would have returned by the time the baby came. They'd charted the remaining weeks of Patricia's pregnancy against the expected return of his ship with a sigh of relief.

When they'd found out that Patricia was with child—days before Dr. Wells was scheduled to leave—he'd been upset at missing the majority of her pregnancy. Rose had promised to write to him, to tell him the day-to-day occurrences.

"Take care of her for me," Dr. Isaac Wells had told her in return. "If I can't be there, you'll have to stand in my stead."

Rose was the younger sister; Patricia had always taken care of her. But somehow, that solemn request, made by a brother-in-law that she liked, had only firmed her resolve. If Patricia had always taken care of Rose, that only meant that Rose now had a chance to return the favor.

And so she wrote to Isaac regularly, telling him everything that transpired. She'd reported faithfully every morning when Patricia felt poorly. She'd described the baby's first tentative flutters, barely detectable, up through the more recent kicks that had drummed against Rose's hand. She'd told him all…but it didn't change a thing. Patricia wished her husband would come back before the baby was born, and Isaac wanted the same thing. He was a little more than a week away now. To have the baby come so close to his arrival would be…

…A blessing, Rose told herself firmly. No matter when it came.

So she swallowed what she had been about to say.

"Have you sent for Chillingsworth?" she asked instead.

"Josephs left a few minutes past. He should be back soon."

Mr. and Mrs. Josephs were the married couple that kept house for Patricia—Mrs. Josephs as the maid-of-all-work, and Mr. Josephs as an all-around handyman. In their neighborhood, having two servants was considered an enormous expense; she'd heard someone whisper that Patricia was putting on airs above her station. But then, Patricia's husband was away, and she herself was pregnant.

"Are you scared?" Rose asked. "What does it feel like, a contraction? I did promise to tell Isaac everything when he returned. You have to tell me."

"Oh, I'm not having the contraction any longer—now I just feel…I don't know, a little odd." Patricia gave a deprecating laugh. "Like a bloated duck on the verge of being popped. But that hasn't changed since last night."

"Can you walk?"

"Of course I can. How do you think I got to your room? Even bloated ducks can manage a good waddle."

Rose smiled. "Well, labor hasn't altered your sense of humor. It's still dreadful."

"Wait until I have another contraction," Patricia said. "Then I'll have no humor at all. Come and wait with me downstairs?"

Rose dressed swiftly and held her sister's hand on the way down the stairs—even though Patricia tried to wave her off, saying she was perfectly able to walk on her own. Once she'd ensconced her sister in pride of place on the sofa, Rose ran around, lighting lamps, pushing away all the shadows of the night. It was lovely to have something to do. She bustled about, fetching and carrying for her sister—slippers, a warm blanket, chamomile tea, and a crumpet that she toasted over a fire and then piled high with butter and currant jelly.

"Mmm," Patricia said, closing her eyes. "Won't you have one, too?"

"I was already having the oddest dream when you woke me," Rose said. "I don't need to upset my digestion any further."

"Dream, eh?" Patricia's eyes narrowed. "You weren't dreaming of—"

"I dreamed I was being chased by a heap of numbers," Rose intervened.

Patricia choked, almost laughing. "You would."

Yes, someone had been laughing in her dream. Almost like that. Friendly laughter, the mirthful burble of someone who knew all Rose's faults and loved her anyway.

It had been too deep a laugh for Patricia, and not merry enough to sound like her mother. Her father's laugh was more of a rumble. And yet it had seemed familiar.

The answer came to Rose as her sister took another bite of crumpet. Mr. Shaughnessy laughed like that.

She'd been avoiding thinking about him. Despite his protestations, she knew exactly what he was doing. This was how men like him seduced women like her: step by careful step, wearing away at her inhibitions one by one.

She had no illusions that her innocence would protect her; innocence was for a different class of women altogether. Rose was a shopkeeper's daughter; she was a woman who worked for a living herself. The well-to-do men who could command society's respect usually thought that women like her existed to serve in whatever capacity they were desired.

She didn't know why she hadn't sent Mr. Shaughnessy on his way. Stupidity, surely. Misplaced romanticism. But this wasn't the time to berate herself.

As her sister took yet another bite of crumpet, the front door opened. Mr. Josephs entered.

Behind him came Doctor Chillingsworth. The physician's coat was wet with glistening rain; he set an umbrella in the umbrella stand, frowning at it as if it had no business being wet. He took off his gloves and chafed his pale hands together for warmth. Then he looked over at Patricia—seated on the sofa, wrapped in wool blankets, trying not to drip red jelly down her chin—and his expression froze in something that looked alarmingly like a sneer.

The back of Rose's neck prickled. But the doctor shook his head, and that hint of a scoff disappeared from his face.

Maybe she'd imagined it. Maybe he simply didn't like jelly.

Chillingsworth was a tall, elderly fellow. He always had an air about him that Rose disliked. It was not exactly disdain; it only smacked mildly of disapproval.

She tried to tell herself she was seeing things that weren't there. He'd come so highly recommended after all. Before he'd retired to civilian practice, he'd spent thirty years as a naval physician. Maybe that air of his was nothing more than residual military discipline.

Patricia's husband didn't have that air—but then, he was only thirty-two. Maybe, she thought dubiously, it took years to develop.

Chillingsworth took off his galoshes, an outer coat, a scarf, and finally, a blue-striped hat. He came forward.

The examination was brief, almost cursory. Patricia's eyes squeezed shut and her breath hissed when he set his stethoscope against her belly. The metal must have been ice cold. But she didn't complain.

The doctor straightened after he'd finished. "Well," he said. "I was roused from bed for nothing."

Patricia blinked.

"Mrs. Wells is having false labor pains," he announced.

At first, Rose had no idea who he was addressing—the room at large, perhaps?—until she followed his line of sight to Mr. Josephs, who was doing his best to wipe up the water that had splashed in the entryway when they had arrived.

How odd of him to talk of Patricia's health with the servant. But then, people sometimes made that mistake. Mr. Josephs may have been a servant, but he was the only man—the only *white* man—in the household, and people often got confused or uncomfortable as a result. It never did to make a fuss about it. They'd all feel better if they just imagined Chillingsworth making pronouncements to the room.

"It is not yet her time," Chillingsworth said. "The baby has not even turned, and she is not dilated. Women like her are often given to dramatics. Next time, make sure the contractions are coming closer together before sending for me in the middle of the night." He glanced back at the entrance. "In the cold rain."

"Yes, Doctor Chillingsworth," Patricia said contritely. "I'm sorry. It's my first time, and I don't know what to expect."

"Humph."

"Would you like a cup of tea to warm up?" Rose offered.

"I'd like my bed," Doctor Chillingsworth said curtly. He stalked back to the entry without looking at her, stamped into his heavy galoshes, and gathered up his things. He muttered to himself as he wound his scarf about his neck. Then he picked up his umbrella, tapped it against the floor—sending droplets of water all over the entryway—and left.

"Dear." Patricia stared after him. "That went...not so well as one would hope."

"That was rude," Rose pointed out.

Patricia waved this away. "Nobody likes being woken in the middle of the night for no reason."

Then maybe he shouldn't be a physician, Rose thought with annoyance. But she did not say that. Instead, she helped her sister to her feet.

"There we are," Patricia said cheerily. "It looks like the bloated duck is here to stay for a few more weeks. And thank God. That means Isaac will be home after all."

⌘ ⌘ ⌘

MISS SWEETLY HAD MOVED their lesson outside on the next day. Stephen didn't know if she'd done so to cool off his imputed ardor, or if she'd just thought it a good idea. Either way, she'd brought them out along the river past the docks. They stood on the water's edge, in the lee of a lamppost that provided not one whit of shelter from the wind.

The people who made their way past reminded him why he had moved to Greenwich. Here, he wasn't the lone Irish interloper in a hoity-toity neighborhood. The nearby docks brought visitors from around the world: lascars from India, midshipmen from the West Indies, swarthy sailors from Portugal...and yes, a goodly number of Irish toiling on ships and in warehouses.

Here, an Irishman standing with a black woman might get an idle second glance, no more. Stephen caught sight of a dock-laborer that he knew from church and gave the man a nod.

The wind gusted around his collar as he did so, bringing in a damp chill off the Thames. Stephen's nose was cold; his hands were going numb. But Miss Sweetly stood beside him, looking as if she were comfortably warming her hands over a fire instead of holding a metal disc in her gloved hands. If *she* didn't feel the cold, he wouldn't, either.

Mrs. Barnstable, by contrast, had given up in the first five minutes. She'd decamped to a nearby tea shop, promising to keep up her vigil from the window.

"To make a measurement by parallax," Miss Sweetly was telling him, "you must be able to determine angles and distances. You can obtain angles on land most simply by using a prismatic compass. Hold the compass—"

He held out his hand; she dumped it unceremoniously into his palm. The metal was cold; he'd been taking notes, and one could hardly wield a pencil while wearing gloves. His breath hissed in.

"Now look through the eyehole, and adjust the prism until the wire contacts the object you are measuring. Read the magnetic angle here."

Someone else might think those words devoid of emotion.

But when she said the word "prism," her lips formed almost a kiss. She reached out and adjusted the compass in his hand, her fingers brushing his palm. And when she looked up after her explanation, she glanced into his eyes and the flow of her words tumbled to a halt. She stood in place, her fingers on the compass, and her eyes widening.

He fascinated her. He was *good* at fascinating women; he didn't even really try to do it. The only difference was that Miss Sweetly thought him both fascinating and frivolous, all at the same time—and he was fairly certain that she was right.

He pulled his hand away and made the measurement, focusing on the building she'd chosen, lining up the wire, making a notation of the angle in his notebook.

"Now to make a second measurement. It must be from a different angle, and a known distance away." She adjusted her spectacles on her nose.

He wondered if her nose was cold. It had to be; they stood in the same wind. But she didn't seem to flinch at all from the weather. He paced off a distance and measured the angle without saying anything. He made a diagram in his little notebook; she came to stand behind him, looking over his shoulder.

"Having you watch me calculate is like…" He paused, searching for an appropriate analogy. "It's like having Beethoven attend a child's first recital on the pianoforte."

She gave a little snort behind him. "I shouldn't think so. There are a few salient differences."

"True. Beethoven isn't female. Beethoven isn't lovely. You're far more disconcerting."

"Mmm. You're not thinking this through. You see, Beethoven isn't alive. I imagine it would be rather more alarming to be visited by the corpse of a composer."

"Does that make him a decomposer?"

She let out a startled choking noise.

Stephen smiled to himself. "I suppose the analogy does rather break down upon examination." He subtracted the magnetic angles and started on the calculation of the triangles. She watched him in silence for a little longer.

"I don't understand why you want me to teach you about astronomy," she said.

"I don't want you to teach me astronomy." As he spoke, he flipped the slide and consulted the trigonometric tables. "I want you to teach me to see the world the way you do."

"How do I see the world?" she asked in puzzlement.

"If I knew, I wouldn't need to learn, would I?" He shrugged. "But I know how you see me. You think I'm an outrageous flirt, a frivolous fellow who thinks of nothing beyond the next joke."

"And you're going to tell me there's more to you?" She sounded dubious.

"If there is, I can't see it myself. But I do wonder sometimes if you might." He shoved the slide over a few inches, read a number off the bottom scale, and marked it down.

"Are you trying to intrigue me by hinting at hidden depths, Mr. Shaughnessy?"

He shrugged. "Why would I? I don't even have hidden shallows. I am very much as you see."

"No hidden traumas, no childhood disappointments, or lingering resentments?"

"Not a one. Oh. Wait. I suppose I do have one. When I was twelve, I was whipped at the stake for rabble rousing."

She turned to him, blinking. "How dreadful."

He dropped his voice, beckoning her closer. She leaned in despite herself. "Do you want to know what I thought when the lash landed? Shall I disclose the solemn vow I made?"

She made no answer, but her eyes sparkled with the light of curiosity.

He bent his head to hers. "I thought: Ouch."

She waited, holding still, as if expecting more.

"That's it. I'm finished. 'Ouch.' Never get whipped as punishment if you can help it, Miss Sweetly. I don't recommend it."

"Thank you," she said solemnly. "I'll keep that in mind." But she bit her lip as she spoke, and he could tell she was suppressing a smile.

He lined up the last numbers on the slide. "It's two hundred and fifty-seven, by the way," he told her.

"Two hundred and fifty-seven what?"

"Feet. To that building over there."

She blinked, as if only now remembering that she was giving him a lesson. "I had judged it at two hundred and fifty-four," she said slowly.

"Ah. Drat."

"But given that your measurement of distance was done by pacing off the length, your answer is certainly within the margin of error." She smiled at him. "Well done. Now should you like to try something difficult?"

"That wasn't difficult? There were sines. And arctangents. I didn't think any problem should be thought easy if it involved arctangents."

"Hush, you great big baby." She shook her head, but she was smiling at him. "All you had to do was look up a number in a table. Was that too difficult for you?"

"A great and mighty table, ringed by fearsome logarithms, with their terrible, terrible…" He trailed off. "Oh, very well. Set me another problem, Miss Sweetly. My resolve is firm and my angles are acute. But beware—if I have to draw another diagram, things may become graphic."

She raised her hands in surrender. "No more mathematical jokes," she said in horror.

"Why? Afraid we might go off on…a *tangent?*"

"It's not that." She bit her lip. "Mathematics are a serious business, for one. And your jokes are terrible, for another."

"I can't help myself." He winked at her. "I was born under an unfortunate sine."

One hand went to her hip. "Mr. Shaughnessy, must I eject you from the pier?"

"Oh, I should think not. Not unless you make me use calculus. I'm afraid my calculus jokes are derivative."

She groaned. "Does your adoring public know that Stephen Shaughnessy, Actual Man, makes truly terrible puns?"

"Sadly, no. I keep trying to put them in my columns, but Free—my editor; that's Frederica Marshall-Clark—keeps taking them out." He made a face.

"Have you finished your little spate of jocularity, Mr. Shaughnessy?" Her words might have sounded harsh, but she was suppressing a smile. "I had intended to set you a problem, if you recall."

"Of course. Go ahead."

"Do you see that ferry?"

"The one in the middle of the Thames?" It was surrounded by choppy waters.

"That very one. Figure out how far away it is, if you please. But here's the catch—this time, no pacing off the distances. In fact, you're not allowed to move your feet at all. You may move your hand a quarter of an inch—no further."

"But the ferry's moving."

"So it is."

"Very well, then." He took out the compass, peered through it…

"May I move my feet over to the railing, just to set the compass down?"

"No," she told him with a calm smile.

It was impossible to hold his hand steady enough.

He blew out a breath. "But the needle in the prism is vibrating. I can't get an accurate read on the angle, and if I can only move my hand a quarter inch, I shall need a very accurate read."

As if to emphasize this, a cart rumbled past and the needle trembled.

She smiled at his dismay. "So you can't do it."

"Did I say that? I can. Of course I can."

He tried stabilizing his hand against his other arm, then holding the compass between thumb and forefinger. The wind picked up, making his grip all the more tenuous—and his fingers even colder. He managed to get an almost decent read once—he thought—but by the time he'd moved his hand the allowed quarter inch and tried to stabilize the needle once more, the ferry had moved so much that the first number was useless.

She watched his struggles with a beatific smile. And that was what finally tipped him off. If the problem were *possible*, she'd be aggravated that he was doing it wrong.

"Miss Sweetly," he said straightening, "would you set me an impossible problem just to watch me struggle with it?"

She put one hand over her heart. "How could you say such a thing? You must think me needlessly cruel."

"No. Of course not. But—"

She smiled. "Good. I should hate you to be deceived as to my character."

He let the compass fall to his side. "Miss Sweetly. You're mocking me. I'm absolutely delighted."

And he was. Every day he spent with her brought her more and more out of her nervousness. The more he saw of her, the better he liked her, and he'd hardly needed to like her better.

She looked away, with a little smile on her face. "Let's go join Mrs. Barnstable. I could use some tea; I'm a little cold."

A little cold. Just a little cold. He shook his head. She set off in the direction of the tea shop and he followed.

"I actually wasn't trying to be mean," she told him as they walked. "I was trying to illustrate a point. The closest stars are trillions of miles away. Even if we took our observations of a star from opposite sides of the globe, we'd only manage a few thousand miles of distance between the two points. I was generous giving you a quarter inch to measure the angle."

He nodded and opened the tea shop door for her. Welcome warmth from the coal stove inside hit him.

But she stopped just inside the shop, and he realized that her glasses had fogged up. She took them off, cleaning them carefully, and then set them on her nose once more. She gave him a suspicious look, as if daring him to laugh at her.

Not a chance. He was taken with a sudden fantasy of fogging them himself, of leaning into her and…

Mrs. Barnstable waved to them as they entered, but she was already seated at a table with another woman, with whom she was gossiping.

Stephen gestured Rose into a seat at the table next to Mrs. Barnstable. "So how is astronomical parallax calculated, then?"

Her eyes brightened. "If we measure the angle of a star in the sky twice yearly, taking into account…" She trailed off, waving her hand, then resumed, "…all the various factors we must consider, then we can have two measurements that are far more than a few thousand miles apart."

"Ah. That is clever."

And it was. A year ago, he'd never have guessed that he would find it all so fascinating. That was before he'd seen her get excited about it. Her eyes lit; her hands gestured. She looked like…like…

Why had he never realized how inadequate all analogies were for women in the throes of utter fascination? She looked like a woman talking about astronomical parallax, and that made her brilliantly beautiful.

"So it really is the same concept as measuring buildings from across the Thames, more or less," she told him. "If I gave you two such measurements, Mr. Shaughnessy, could you determine the distance of a star?"

"I think so."

She rattled off a pair of numbers. He began to calculate—and realized that he'd boasted too soon. He looked up to see her watching him with that same beatific smile on her face. A girl came with tea and biscuits; Miss Sweetly poured, but didn't say anything else.

"Miss Sweetly."

"Yes, Mr. Shaughnessy?" she said innocently.

"I spoke too soon. I can't do a thing until I know the distance between the two points of measurement."

"Ah," she said with a long, drawn-out sigh. "That's so."

"It's twice the distance between the earth and the sun—but how is one to measure that? Let a giant piece of string trail behind the earth as it passes, and then reel it back in? I have no idea. I think you must enjoy setting me impossible problems."

"I'm merely making you comfortable with the notion of failure," she told him, looking down. "When it comes to me, you should expect to fail. Often."

He set his chin on his hands. "I'd rather fail at you than succeed at anyone else."

She went utterly still. Her jaw squared; she glanced to one side, ascertaining that Mrs. Barnstable was not listening, and then she looked back at him.

"Too much," she told him. "When you say extravagant things like that, I remember that this is all a game to you. You'd do much better if you used less effusive praise."

"I'll remember that, if I ever decide to seduce you." He picked up his teacup and took a healthy swallow of warm liquid. "But it's rather ironic, don't you think? You were about to tell me how to measure the distance between the earth and the sun without using string. You can imagine numbers larger than I have ever dreamed about. And yet you can't grasp hold of the possibility that maybe, just maybe, you really have brought me to my knees."

She pulled back, giving her head a fierce shake. "Don't be ridiculous. Women like me don't—"

He set his hand on the table, interrupting this thought. "My father was a stable master," he told her. "My mother was a seamstress. I've done very well for myself, but don't imagine that I'm one of those gentlemen who look down on you."

She looked away, dropping a lump of sugar into her tea.

"As for women like you... I don't believe I have ever met a woman like you. Tell me, Miss Sweetly. How did you become the sort of woman who calculated cometary orbits?"

She picked up a teaspoon. "I've always been exceptional at maths. I do mean always. When I was four, we still lived with my grandfather in Liverpool. He owned a shop there, and one day, a man came to the register with a basket of goods. I knew what the total would be, so I said it aloud." She shrugged. "My grandfather made a game of it. I could add a basket at a glance. Grown men would come to watch. A great many of them. By the time I left, there would be a crowd there every day."

Her lips twitched as if she'd tasted something unpleasant.

"Miss Sweetly, that sounds like a hidden depth."

"Unlike you, I have never claimed not to have them." She dipped the teaspoon in her tea and slowly stirred the brown liquid. "It made me uncomfortable, all those people watching. And the things they would say... I was very glad when my father came to London to start his own emporium. I wasn't on display any longer, not until my father tried to have me learn deportment." Rose smiled. "It didn't work so well—I didn't like the idea of performing in society. Eventually, on Patricia's advice, he bribed me to pay attention by offering me tutoring in higher mathematics."

She was still stirring her tea even though the sugar must have long since dissolved.

"So you see, it's nothing, really. Just a little trick I do, something that brings me some amusement."

"Right," he said skeptically. "Just a little trick. Tell me, Miss Sweetly. How *does* one calculate the distance between the earth and the sun?"

She looked up, her eyes brightening. "Oh, so many ways. But there's really only one astronomical event that allows us to make a truly accurate measurement. We can observe the exact time it takes for Venus to cross between the earth and the sun. Two such observations taken at different latitudes would give the most exact distance possible."

"You sound as if this has not yet been done."

"It was attempted before, but there were difficulties…" She caught his eye. "Never mind the difficulties. The entire astronomical community has been preparing for this upcoming transit. Britain alone has twelve stations manned around the world for just this event."

"A lot of to-do about one little number," he teased.

"But I've already told you!" She sounded shocked. "It's not just one little number. It is the only yardstick we have to measure the universe with, and we don't know how long it is! If we knew that distance accurately, we'd know not just how far the stars were, but we could deduce the distance of all the planets in the solar system. We'd then know their mass, which would allow us to test our measurements of the gravitational constant, see if this so-called ether exists…" She trailed off once again, looking up at him. Slowly, the light drained from her eyes. Watching her slide back into self-consciousness was like watching a candle flame flicker in a sudden wind and then go out.

"Oh," she said in a small voice. "You were teasing me."

"No," Stephen said. "I was proving a point."

She flinched. "What, that you can set me to babbling?"

"You keep looking for dark, complicated reasons, Miss Sweetly. I don't complicate. I'm simple. I like hearing you talk about the solar system. If I didn't like it, I wouldn't ask."

"You can't pretend you're a mathematical enthusiast. I've seen you wrestle with an arctangent, Mr. Shaughnessy, and I wasn't sure you would win."

Stephen leaned toward her. "It's because your enthusiasm is a contagion. You look at the sky and see not pretty little lights, but a cosmos to be discovered. If I could listen to you talk and *not* smile in appreciation, I would be an unfeeling brute. And you think the praise I give you is over-extravagant? One of these days, you'll realize how much I'm truly restraining myself."

She stole a glance over at him—one that was both wary and hopeful all at once.

"So tell me," he said. "When will Venus next intervene between us and the sun? The way you were speaking, it sounds as if it will be soon."

Her fingers fumbled with a teaspoon. "It's just days from now," she told him. "On the sixth of December at almost precisely two in the afternoon."

"And naturally, you'll be observing this event."

"Oh…" She looked down again. "From here in London, only about half of the transit will be visible, and that only weather permitting. The sun will set before it's finished. I have a piece of smoked glass that I'll be using to observe—which is hardly ideal, the planet is so small, and…" She trailed off.

"And I don't understand. You work at an observatory. Surely you'd have access to better observational tools than smoked glass."

"I'm not one of the astronomers," she said in a low voice. "I'm just a computer. There's only so much space, and everyone else wants to see it."

Just. She still didn't believe him.

"Well, then." He gave her his best smile. "Next time, you must attach yourself to one of the scientific teams going to…where was it you said? Bermuda?"

But she was shaking her head again. "No, no."

"You think you can't?" He paused, considering her. "The fact that you are female poses some difficulties. The race, I assume, is also a hindrance?"

She nodded.

"But then, those must be overshadowed by the utter brilliance of your mind."

She smiled, but it was a shaky, wavering smile. "It's not that, Mr. Shaughnessy. I mean, it *is* that, but in this case, it wouldn't help." She swallowed. "You see, the transit of Venus is a rare astronomical event—exceedingly rare. There is no next time, not in my life. It won't happen again until June of the year 2004." She gave him a sad shake of her head. "So yes, Mr. Shaughnessy. I'm not one of the people who will watch this happen in all its glory. Women like me will have to content ourselves with glimpsing the phenomenon in smoked glass."

Stephen hadn't known what he intended when he first approached Dr. Barnstable. But looking at her now, her head bent, disclaiming all importance... Now, for the first time, he knew what he wanted.

Chapter Four

"ROSE," PATRICIA SAID THE NEXT MORNING, "I particularly think you should read this." She slid a paper across the breakfast table to sit alongside Rose's teacup.

Rose looked up from her toast to see the *Women's Free Press* opened to Mr. Shaughnessy's latest column.

"I thought you didn't want to encourage me in this."

"This isn't encouragement," Patricia said gravely. "It's a reminder of who he is, what he is. He's flirting with you…"

Rose felt her cheeks heat. Patricia didn't know the half of it.

"…and at the same time, he's carrying on like this, in public. In a *newspaper*."

Rose had read a good number of Mr. Shaughnessy's columns. She had an idea of the sort of things he wrote. She doubted anything he could write would shock her—and if Patricia only knew the sorts of things he was saying to her face, she'd know that she would need a more powerful arsenal than a few lines in a newspaper. Still, Rose dutifully picked up the paper.

Dear Man, she read. *I am sorry to say that I have spent the last five years in a madhouse. My uncle and guardian had me put there when I refused to marry my cousin. I passed my time in that horrible place by making a list of all the things I would do if ever I were released. Now he is dead and I am free, but I find I cannot bring myself to do even one of them. How does one go about setting oneself free?*

—Not Mad.

Rose swallowed hard and read on.

Dear Not Mad,

Normally I approach my columns with a certain amount of jocularity. (Never tell this to my readers; they would never believe it.) But your situation has moved me to seriousness. You must work yourself up to your desires, bit by bit. Before you can dance on your uncle's grave (I assume this to be on your list), you must first visit it and stand upon the grass. On the next visit, be sure to tap your toe and hum a ditty. Before you know it, you'll be waltzing in the cemetery.

Should you need a dancing partner, consider yours truly.

Sincerely,
Stephen Shaughnessy
Actual Man

"You see?" Patricia said. "He's flirting—publicly—with another woman. That's the sort of man he is. Just keep that in mind the next time you encounter him." She nodded as if she had proven a point.

Rose shook her head. It wasn't flirting, no more than the time he'd done the *Actual Man* thing to Mrs. Barnstable had been flirting. It was…kind of him, in a sweet, outrageous sort of way. It hurt to read it, not because she thought him unfaithful, but because she could hear him in it, all of him.

I don't have hidden shallows, he'd told her. Maybe he didn't. She suspected that if she judged him by his column, she would see…

A man who offered to dance with a woman who had been badly wounded. A man who mocked other men when they made too much of their own importance. A man who wished to make others laugh, even when they suffered. She had never looked at him and seen a bad man, and the more she looked, the deeper she fell.

That, perhaps, made him the most dangerous specimen of all.

He liked people. He liked *her.* She suspected he'd told her the simple truth: He wasn't *trying* to seduce her.

He was just succeeding at it.

⌘ ⌘ ⌘

"This will be our last lesson," Rose said, when Mr. Shaughnessy had settled himself into her office two days later. "There is only so much you need to learn, and after tomorrow I shall be flooded with work. We'll have data from the transit of Venus—and once we have that, there will be star charts to update, and I shall be up to my ears in calculations. I shan't have time for you any longer."

Mrs. Barnstable looked up at that, but she had a report to type for her husband, and the noise of the typewriter drowned out their conversation.

The truth was that Rose should never have made time for Mr. Shaughnessy. He was… *Charming* was the word she'd used, but charming sounded so sweet, so innocent. And by nature, Mr. Shaughnessy was never innocent.

He was not watching her innocently now.

That was the problem. She knew precisely what was happening to her. She could feel him coaxing her along the path to seduction. He made her forget herself every day she was with him, and one day, she would cross an uncrossable line. So long as he was around her, he would lead her astray.

His lips thinned, but he nodded ever so slightly as if he were accepting her edict.

"You'll still tell me what you're doing when we meet on the street," he said. "And now I'll understand it better."

She shook her head. "I don't think I should."

No; that was too wishy-washy. The clattering of Mrs. Barnstable's machine was beginning to annoy Rose.

"In fact, I know I mustn't."

"Aw, Rose." He looked into her eyes. "You know I love it when you talk Sweetly to me."

Her throat seemed to close at those words. She felt hoarse, almost ill. Her heart was pounding and her head seemed light. But this was no illness; she wanted more of it.

Therein lay her problem. He'd told her that her enthusiasm was contagious.

His lack of innocence, then, was a raging plague, and she was infected. The smallest glance in his direction sent her into an internal tizzy—the flash of his eyes, a glimpse of his wrist when one of his cuffs pulled up. The sight of him gave her ideas, and she didn't need to be having *ideas* about him.

Once she had it in her head that he might do things to her, she could not help but imagine those things. Kisses, and not just on the lips or the hand, but on her neck, her inner wrist, up her elbow. He might give her caresses, too—slow, languid, full-body caresses. He didn't have to seduce her; she was doing all the work of seduction on her own.

"Come, Mr. Shaughnessy," she said briskly. "I'm sure you dream of more important things than listening to me ramble on. I don't wish to be a way station on your way to bigger and better." She looked down. "I have enjoyed—rather too much—spending this time with you. But I think I'll be better off if our time together draws to a close."

He took this in silence. His lips compressed into an almost angry line, and he looked away.

"Here," she said. "I've set you some…some problems to work. Just a little parallax." She actually choked as she spoke, as if she might cry over mathematics.

Better that. Better to cry over maths than a man, especially a rogue like this one. He'd scarcely even exerted himself and already she found herself watching his fingers, hoping he might crook one of them at her…and fearing that if he did, she'd come running.

He took the sheet from her and began to work.

"You know," he said, "I realized last night that you were granting me a signal honor when you let me use your slide rule. Thank you."

He didn't sound as if he were making fun of her. She glanced suspiciously at him.

"I don't dream of bigger and better," he said, making his first notation on the page. "I told you: I'm appallingly simple. There is no grand design."

"You're a novelist. And a columnist. There's nothing simple about you."

"Yes," he said. "I'm exceedingly clever and exceedingly outrageous. But that doesn't make me exceedingly devious."

"But you must have had some plan in order to ascend the heights so swiftly."

He smirked. "Here is the extent of my planning. When I was fifteen, I realized I was a poor Irish Catholic in England, a country with an excess of poor Irish Catholics. My only real skill was a talent for outraging others. Either I had to stamp out my only source of genius in order to have a go at making a living in the most menial fashion, or I had to indulge it to the fullest and hope for the best." He shrugged. "Here I am. For the next few years, I shall be in demand enough to command a thousand pounds per book from my publisher. By the time that's dried up—and the public's capacity for any brand of outrage always dries up—I'll have enough saved that I won't have to care. See? There is no grand plan. No meteoric dreams. Just a dislike for manual labor and a talent for annoying others."

She sniffed.

"You, on the other hand…"

She shook her head. "We are not talking of me."

"You, I wager, do not dream timid dreams. You walk with your head in the clouds."

"Oh, no. The clouds are in the troposphere. My thoughts lie well beyond the mesosphere."

"Precisely. So tell me, Miss Sweetly. What is it *you* see for yourself, after you send me on my way? What is your grand plan?"

Behind them, Mrs. Barnstable changed a page in her typewriter. Rose flushed and looked away. "There is no grand plan. My father is on the board of the *African Times*. It has been their mission for the last decades to see to the elevation of the race. They've sponsored a number of medical students in their work, starting with Africanus Horton." She couldn't look him in the eyes. "Patricia—my sister—married one of those students. They met over dinner, took one look at each other…and that was the end of it. Everyone expects that I'll marry one of the two students arriving in the next year." Rose traced a trailing vine on her skirt. "I suppose I do, too."

"And is that what you want?" he asked in a low voice. "To marry a medical student on scholarship? To have his children and to keep his home?"

"I am not opposed to marriage. And yes, I should like children." She still couldn't bring herself to look at him.

"Will your husband let you spend your days in computation? Will he listen to you talk of parallax and the transit of Venus? Or will he expect you to subside into compliance, to set your slide rule aside until it is dusty and warped?"

Her chin went up. "How do you suppose I met Dr. Barnstable? He's also on the board of the *African Times*—he was stationed in Cape Town, and didn't like some of the things he saw. He heard about this ridiculous talent I had, and next thing I knew, he was pleading with my father to let me work with him. I know for a fact that there are men in this world who will allow a woman her interests."

"True. But would they adore you for yours? Where others see numbers and charts, you see a universe, vast and mighty. You can see the face of the cosmos in a few dancing lights. You shouldn't have to trade the stars in the sky for a home and a marriage and babies."

She let out a shaky breath.

"I admit," he said, "it took me longer than one look at dinner. It took me five or six looks. But then, I cannot see five trillion miles away."

Her heart was pounding heavily. "Mr. Shaughnessy."

"I'm a clever fellow," he went on. "I know I'm not your heart's desire. I'm too outrageous, too frivolous to be the sort of man you dream about."

She couldn't speak. She didn't dare tell him what she truly longed for. If she did, he'd use it against her.

Mrs. Barnstable, oblivious to this entire exchange, pulled the last page from her machine. "Miss Sweetly, I'm just running these down to Dr. Barnstable, if that's all right with you."

No. Rose needed to say *no*. She couldn't be alone with Mr. Shaughnessy, not even for so much as a minute. Especially not now.

"Of course, Mrs. Barnstable," she heard herself say.

"I know I'm not your heart's desire," he said again in a low voice as soon as Mrs. Barnstable had quitted the room, "but I can still give you yours."

She looked up. "What do you know of my heart's desire?"

Looking into his eyes was a mistake. He gave her a smile—not a low, cunning smile, or a clever smile that hinted at seduction. It was a warm, welcoming smile—the sort that made her think she had come home.

"I know what you want. It shows."

She wanted him, impossible rake that he was. She wanted him in love with her, faithful to her. Even she knew that was too much to ask.

"It shows?" she asked in a low voice.

"It does." He gave her a duck of his head. "Miss Sweetly, I beg of you—that you will accept from me this one thing."

Her heart pounded.

He stood. She looked wildly around the room—but with Mrs. Barnstable gone, there was no one to see. Nobody would see him coming toward her. Nobody would detect the look in his eye, that bright light that froze her in her seat.

He got on one knee before her. She couldn't think, couldn't imagine what to say or how to say it. He wouldn't really ask her to marry him—not now, *ever,* and even if he did, surely he wouldn't mean it. Men promised things to women like her all the time, and never meant a word they said.

But the thing he took from his pocket was not a ring. It was a bit of card stock, printed with a decorative border. He handed it to her; she took it. Stamped on the front were the words *Admit One.* Beneath that, there was only an address.

"What is this?" she asked in confusion.

"That?" He smiled smugly, as if he had just done something very clever. "That is your heart's desire, Miss Sweetly: a ticket to the best viewing in all of Greenwich of the transit of Venus. Courtesy of... Well, that would be *me.*"

If anyone had asked Rose about the things she wanted, watching the transit of Venus would assuredly have been on her list. Not the first item there, nor the second...but high on the list nonetheless.

But it wasn't the thought of astronomy that had her breath catching in her lungs. It was that he'd obtained this as a present. It was the most thoughtful gift she'd ever received. And he'd been the one to think of it.

"It's a very exclusive viewing," he said, "from one of the highest points in Greenwich itself. There will be a great many steps up, and there won't be a fire in the viewing room for warmth, so take that into account when dressing."

There was one thing wrong with this. "People will talk if I arrive at an event like this with you."

"Ah." His eyes glittered. "It's a very exclusive gathering. I assure you, nobody will speak of you. Nobody at all. As for me? I promise not to importune you."

Watching the transit of Venus with a handful of people she didn't know would be interesting. Delightful, even. But her heart's desire, even if it was only for an afternoon...

...was to have him truly care for her. It might be temporary. It might be foolish. But if he'd gone to this length, she was more than a whim to him.

He's seducing you, she told herself.

Just this much, she pleaded in return. *Just this far, and after that, I'll venture no further.*

"Oh, very well," she said. But when she looked in his eyes, she couldn't stop from smiling.

Heavens, she was a fool.

⌘ ⌘ ⌘

SHE WAS A FOOL, Rose told herself for the twentieth time in as many hours. She'd been arguing with herself ever since Mr. Shaughnessy had issued his invitation.

She'd argued with herself silently as she told her sister she'd be home the next day no later than four-thirty because she was observing an astronomical event. She had argued with herself all through her computations the next morning. She argued with herself now, at half past one, heading to the address on the card he had given her.

She knew what Mr. Shaughnessy was about; she knew better than to accept an invitation to any event with him, no matter how intellectually engaging it was. She really ought to have insisted on bringing a companion— why hadn't she thought of that earlier?

Oh. Because she was a fool.

But every time she told herself she was a fool, she also remembered what he'd said. *You do not dream timid dreams.*

The address he had given her was not so far from the Royal Observatory; it stood on that same high ground. She wondered, idly, if one of Dr. Barnstable's acquaintances would be present at this viewing party.

He'd promised people wouldn't talk, but how could he know? How could he stop them?

There was a part of her, scarcely buried, that dreamed that he was in love with her. Who thought that no matter how different they might seem in comparison with each other, they would get on well together. She could see them fitting into each other's lives so comfortably. He lived near the Royal Observatory; she could continue going in the mornings. In the afternoons, they might walk together, and he could tell her about his work for a change. And at nights…

That was where it all broke down. She could imagine their nights alone all too well. But whenever she tried to make herself imagine going out in company with him, she remembered who she was and how she'd be received.

You do not dream timid dreams.

She didn't *want* to dream timid dreams. She just knew the truth: She didn't belong in his sphere, and women like her were not invited to join men like him in matrimony. The only way she would have a man like him was if he did seduce her. They could deal with each other very well alone. It was only when she imagined...oh, anyone else at all around them that it all fell to pieces.

The address he had given her was situated on Crooms Hill. When she was almost there, she realized that he was not directing her to a rooftop viewing at a stately, private home; there was only one place high enough for viewing the transit of Venus.

That place was a church. Not just any church, but a Roman Catholic church—a place she had often passed but never entered. If he'd been invited to view the transit of Venus there, he must attend regularly—regularly enough that they'd know him.

Somehow, that thought seemed entirely incompatible with the Mr. Shaughnessy that she knew. The Mr. Shaughnessy she knew was outrageous. He took part in all sorts of immoral acts. He wrote columns that hinted at things that Patricia had refused to explain, and that she'd had to figure out as best as she could on her own. And that was nothing to the gossip that linked him to woman after woman.

It was impossible to think of him as a regular churchgoer.

And yet he'd invited her here. She came up to the graceful building roofed in slate and dressed in Caen stone. A tall spire wound its way up to the heavens, terminating in a cross.

Even Mr. Shaughnessy would not seduce her in a church.

Would he?

She was staring at the church in something like dismay when he came out the front doors and strode to her side. "There you are," he said.

"Here I am," she heard herself repeating. "You *did* promise not to importune me, didn't you?"

"Ah, but I'm sure you've already determined the loophole in that." He winked at her. "I never said anything about what you could do to me. Come along."

He did not take her into the chancel. She caught a glimpse of a marble statue of a lady, a gold-plated ship beside her, before he conducted her into a back way.

"Mr. Shaughnessy," she said, balking a little. "Where are we going?"

"Up the turret, of course," he said. "We're ascending the spire."

He stopped in front of a wooden door and took out a key ring.

"Where did you get that?"

The door swung open onto a dark, stone staircase.

"Father Wineheart," he said. "He likes me."

She had nothing to say to that. There was something odd about this, something dreadfully strange about that darkened staircase…

"Mr. Shaughnessy," she said, "do you mean to tell me that there is nobody else watching the transit of Venus with us? Nobody at all?"

He stopped, raising an eyebrow at her. "I did tell you it was very exclusive, and that nobody would talk."

She had thought he meant that the party was discreet. Maybe she hadn't let herself dwell on it overmuch. Maybe that had been purposeful. She *was* a fool. If she had thought more clearly, she would have known. And if she had known—even as foolish as she was being now—she wouldn't have come.

"Mr. Shaughnessy." She put her hands on her hips. "I had assumed there would be mixed company, that I wasn't going to be alone with you as the sun set. It would be horribly improper for me to follow you into…this."

He paused and looked at her. For a moment, his nose wrinkled. She wished she knew what he was thinking. She almost wanted him to charm her into compliance, to convince her to go up with him. She could imagine the whole thing unfolding. How *did* rakes make women lose their minds? Champagne? Madeira?

He'd offer her a glass. She would…

Drat it all. She would say no. But if she let this happen now—if she let him take her alone into a dark spire—she'd let it happen a second time, and then a third. Maybe the fourth time, she'd say yes to the Madeira. By the fifth time, it would be more. She knew how rakes seduced women, and she knew she was more than halfway there. She'd promised herself that she'd only go this far and no further…and if she didn't keep that promise now, she might as well give up and give in.

She swallowed hard and looked away. "I'm sorry. I'm truly sorry. But I can't go alone with you into a deserted turret."

"Aw, Rose."

No. He couldn't plead with her. He'd break her down.

"Not even for the transit of Venus," she said. Her voice broke.

But when she looked over at him, he wasn't looking at her beseechingly. He was looking at her with another expression on his face—one she couldn't understand.

She didn't want to let herself understand. "I'd better go." She turned to do just that.

"Wait. Rose."

Against her own better judgment, she stopped. She knew she shouldn't. She knew he'd make her laugh, that he'd put her at ease. He scarcely had to convince her at all; she wanted to be convinced so desperately.

He took a step toward her, and then another, standing so close that he might have set his fingers on her chin. She could feel herself opening to him, her eyes shining up at him. He could kiss her right here, in view of the chancel, and she might let him.

But he didn't. Instead, he pitched his voice low. "Do you think I would do that to you?"

"I don't think you'd have to try too hard." Already she was trying to persuade herself without any effort on his part at all. She had only to keep quiet, to keep her distance. She might watch the transit; then she'd go down the stairs, and nobody would ever be the wiser. If she never did it again…

No. That sort of thinking was precisely how girls like her ended up ruined.

His gaze slipped to her lips. "That isn't what I meant." He inhaled sharply, and then held out the key ring. "Right, then. The door to the spire is opened by this little key here, the copper one."

She blinked at him in confusion.

"You've got twelve minutes until the transit starts. There's a great many stairs, but if you hurry, they shouldn't prove to be much problem. There's an excellent view of the river once you get to the turret."

She shook her head. "What are you saying?"

"This is a rare astronomical event," he told her. "It won't happen again until the year 2004. Do you really think I would let you miss it? If you can't go with me, go by yourself." He leaned against the wall. "I'll wait here. I need to get the keys back to Father Wineheart when you're finished."

"You're really not going to come?"

"Did I not just say that? Go. Hurry. You don't want to miss it."

He gave her a wave of his hands, urging her through the door onto the dark staircase. She started up. The stair was cold and just a little musty, but she couldn't think of that.

She had come, expecting him to wear down her every defense—and hoping, almost, that he might succeed.

And…he hadn't even tried. No jokes. He'd taken no little jabs at her when she'd balked. He'd just handed her the keys and told her to go. He hadn't tried to wheedle or charm her, and if he'd made even the slightest effort, he could have brought her around. She knew it all too well. And Mr. Shaughnessy, Actual Man, expert that he was with the human female, must have known it, too.

It was almost as if he cared what she wanted. She came to the topmost landing on the stair turret. Her calves were already a little warm from the exertion; the air around her had become colder. She could see out the little rectangular window, down onto the river, over to a sun dipping lazily in the sky. Clouds far away over London threatened, but they'd not be here in time to block her view. She took the key ring out, found the copper key, and put it reluctantly in the door that led to the spire.

Eight minutes until the transit started. Eight minutes until she stood, watching it alone, with her heart still back down the stone stairs.

Rose inhaled. And then—stupidly—she started back down the stairs, slowly at first, and then faster and faster, until her shoes pattered heavily against the stairs, taking them two and then three at a time. When she reached the final landing, she was going so fast that her feet skittered against the smooth stone. She held up her hands to stop from slamming into a wall, and then she pushed off once again.

She went out the little wooden door. He was sitting on a bench nearby. He had a little book out and he was reading.

"Stephen." She'd never called him by his Christian name before, and hadn't intended to do so now. It had simply slipped out.

He looked up. She hadn't understood herself why she'd come back. Not until she saw his face. He caught sight of her. His eyes widened and he burst into a smile, a lovely, brilliant smile that seemed to cast light throughout the darkening corridor. She felt an answering smile spread shyly across her face.

"Rose," he said. "What are you still doing here? There's a transit about to start."

"I can't watch it without you," she said. "I won't enjoy it."

He looked at her.

"Come now," she said. "Hurry. If I miss this because of you..."

He stood. And then, very slowly, with a broadening smile, he came toward her.

Chapter Five

ROSE WAS SWIFT. She had a head start on Stephen, darting up the stairs. By the time he'd entered the stair turret, he saw only a swirl of pink skirts as she turned, already on the landing ahead of him. He followed after, his mind a maelstrom of confusion.

She stopped halfway up the next short flight of stairs and turned to him. Her eyes were shining from the exercise—and then she reached back to him, holding out her hand.

"Well?" she said. "Come along."

He stopped dead. For a moment, he wasn't sure what she intended. Slowly, he climbed the steps that separated them until he stood just below her. That brought him on eye-level with her.

He held out his hand, palm up.

She took it, folding it in her own. "Hurry up," she said.

Then she took off again. He was jogging up the stairs beside her, hand in hand. She had a smile on her face. Her fingers squeezed his, and he squeezed them back.

They came to the top of the turret. She fumbled the keys out, unlocking the final door. There were no easy stairs up the spire. Instead, a wooden ladder sat at the base, climbing to a final platform.

"Climb quickly," she told him.

He did. He could feel her on the ladder behind him even though he couldn't see her—feel her in the vibration of the ladder, sense her in his tingling nerves.

He came to the top, pulled himself onto the platform, and crouched down and held out his hand. She took it, and he helped her up.

There were two windows in the spire. One faced northeast; the other— the one he'd spent all morning setting the apparatus up in—faced south and west. She dropped his hand, inhaling, going to that one.

"Mr. Shaughnessy." Her voice shook. "Did you do this?"

He'd had to talk with Barnstable about how to manage it.

"Well. Yes. I did."

One couldn't look at the sun directly, not without risking damage to the eyes. But with the proper telescope lens, it was no difficulty at all.

"You've mounted an entire theodolite telescope in the window. How did you get..." She shook her head in wonder. "No, never mind that. I can tell how. No one who owned a theodolite telescope would willingly loan it to you, not with the transit today. Never say you bought it just for this."

"As you wish." He smiled. "I won't tell you that I bought it. But..."

She shook her head. "And were no doubt charged treble in light of the transit." She reached out and touched the base lightly, almost reverently.

"Do you have a telescope, Miss Sweetly?"

"No." Her voice was low and reverent. "I don't."

"Well, then. Do you want one?"

"Yes, Mr. Shaughnessy." She bent over it, set her eye to the eyepiece. "I want one very much. But we both know you cannot make a present of this to me. It is too dear."

"Then I won't."

"It seems an extravagant purchase on your part," she said.

He'd had years of scrimping and saving before he'd come to prominence; it was not in his nature to make pointless expenditures. But when the shopkeeper had quoted him the cost of the telescope, he hadn't even blinked.

She was enraptured. The light from the window illuminated her figure, casting a golden glow all around.

"It was worth it," he told her. He would have purchased a score of telescopes just to see the look on her face now.

"But to buy such a thing for a single use... I suppose you can sell it." She trailed her fingers longingly down the tube.

He'd never intended the use to be singular. She adjusted the inclination, her head bent like a woman in prayer.

One day. One day, he hoped she'd look at him with half that amount of emotion, that wonder. One day he'd make her feel just a little breathless.

Today, though...

"I don't understand you," she said, still peering into the telescope. "Surely after going through all the trouble and expense of setting this up, you expected some return on your investment."

"Oh, I have it already," he said nonchalantly.

She glanced up at him.

"I told you," he said. "I just want to give you your heart's desire." Their eyes met, the moment stretching.

She looked back down with a shake of her head. "It must be about time."

He didn't speak. He could see her excitement in the tap of her gloved fingers against the scope, in her breath catching. "It's starting," she said.

Somewhere, a clock tolled the two o'clock hour.

"Come here." She gestured to him.

"I don't want to take your time…"

She made an impatient noise. "It will never again happen in our lives, and you don't want to see it? Don't be ridiculous."

The telescope, fitted with a solar filter, showed the image of the sun clearly—a bright disc the size of a sixpence. A dark spot, the merest speck, had just broached the edge.

He'd never stood so close to her. He could smell the sweet fragrance of rosewater, of something else he couldn't identify, something enticing and lovely. Her shoulder brushed his. If he turned to her now…

He'd distract her, and she'd never forgive him. "How long will this last?"

"Until the sun sets just after four or the clouds intervene."

"Well. Then maybe we can take turns." He gestured her back to the telescope.

She took her place once more. But after a few moments of staring into the eyepiece, she spoke again. "However did you convince Father Wineheart to let you set this whole thing up?"

"He likes me," Stephen said. "Even though he hears my confessions— which I must admit are shocking—he likes me."

"That's not what I meant. Why did he agree?"

"The same reason that Barnstable did. I told him I was writing a book about an astronomer, that I needed a little experience." Stephen shrugged.

She straightened and glanced at him. "When are you going to tell him that you were using that as an excuse to try and seduce a woman? I would not think that a man of the cloth, no matter what his denomination, would acquiesce in such a scheme." Her words were severe, but her tone was light and teasing.

"I told you already. I'm not trying to seduce you." But he couldn't help but smile. "If it happens, it will be a happy side-effect."

She raised an eyebrow.

"But he'll find out when he hears my next confession."

She shook her head, and leaned down once more. "I can't do what you do, you know."

"What do I do?"

She waved a hand—a very general hand-motion that he decoded as *I don't want to say, and I'd be obliged if you inferred it without any more effort on my part.*

"Do you mean that you couldn't write novels?"

She snorted.

"That you couldn't write my columns? You're right, Miss Sweetly. I think you're a little too earnest for them."

"No. You know that's not what I mean. I mean, how do you…do the things you do with women and not fall in love?"

"Ah."

He pushed away from her and looked out the window. The sun was a dusky gold; with his naked eye, he could see no hint that anything extraordinary was taking place.

"That's easy enough to answer. The first time, I did."

She did look up from the telescope at that.

"I was nineteen, which according to some, is rather late to start on such matters. But I'd been concentrating on my studies, and, well…" He shrugged. "I had just started writing for the *Women's Free Press,* and there was some gala event that I was invited to. I met this woman. She was ten years my elder, widowed, and absolutely lovely. I was charmed, delighted, seduced, and I promptly fell head over ears in love." He put his hands in his pockets. "I think it took me a week to propose marriage. She kissed me on the cheek and laughed at me. You see, I was not the sort of man that a woman like her would marry. And she told me why in great detail. I hadn't any money, any station. I was Irish and Catholic. I was too young and far too radical. Women would adore me, she said—and I could offer them a great deal—but I shouldn't expect to marry them."

She did not look up from the telescope. "Mr. Shaughnessy," she said slowly, "that sounds suspiciously like a hidden depth."

He let out a gasp. "You're right. It is!" She wasn't looking at him, but still he played it for all it was worth, setting a hand over his breast. "I *do* have a secret trauma—my many prior love affairs. There can be no sharper pain then to make love to a vast number of women—but I have masterfully accepted it as my due. I soldier on under the burden."

She shook her head. "Are you ever serious?"

"I suppose some other man might have been wounded by that. But I'm like a cashmere jumper: comfortable, soft, and as fabric goes, not much given to wrinkling."

"No wrinkles? Not over even one of them?"

"Aside from the obvious, it was all to my advantage. If one wishes to be a grand, outrageous name in society, one must do a few grand, outrageous things. Absinthe is too dangerous; gambling is too expensive. Opium is a dreadful habit—one has only to look at those in an opium den to know the effect. No; if I was going to be an outrage, I wanted the safest, least expensive vice I could find. So women it was."

Rose inhaled. "Are you telling me that you seduce women as a calculation?"

"It's been mutual. And I don't seduce women—at least not the way you mean it. The Countess of Howder wanted an affair with me to let everyone know she was out of mourning and didn't intend to be a pattern card of propriety. I'm an outrage, and the women who are so placed as to wish to be outrageous, well…" He shrugged. "And besides, I *like* women. I like them a great deal."

She straightened. But instead of upbraiding him, as he'd expected, she gestured to the telescope. "Come take a look."

He did. It was unnerving to not be able to see her—not after what he'd confessed. The dark spot had begun to traverse the sun's disc.

"Aren't there dangers in using women that way?"

"There are. There are also ways to minimize those dangers. Technically, they're also forbidden to me, but…"

A longer pause. "Do you confess those ways to Father Wineheart as well?"

"I confess all my sins."

He could hear her behind him, but with his eye on the disc of the sun, he could not see her. He had no idea if she was outraged or interested, if he'd disgusted her forever or set her mind at ease.

"I can't imagine that. You tell all these salacious details to Father Wineheart, and in turn, he lets you put a telescope in the spire."

"I only moved to this parish three months ago, Rose." He shrugged. "I met you almost the first day I was here. I've had nothing to confess since that moment."

She inhaled behind him, sounding almost shocked. "Nothing at all?"

"Nothing but lust, which he rather expects from a man my age." He straightened, gesturing her back to the telescope. "You'd better take it back, Rose. The clouds are coming in—I'd hate to have you miss anything."

She held his eyes for a long moment. He didn't know what she was seeing, didn't know what she was thinking. She bent back down.

She had to adjust the telescope yet again to track the sun in its descent. She didn't say anything for a while, but he could see her hands nervously tapping against the optical tube. Her breath was uneven.

"Tell me, Mr. Shaughnessy. Is that what you had hoped for from me? To…" She stopped briefly, swallowing, and then continued. "To seduce me and then not fall in love?"

"No," he told her. "I'm tired of having to remind myself that the women who are after me wish only an experience or a reputation and not a lifetime. I'm tired of holding myself back. I'm tired of having to flatten all but the barest hint of affection."

Her breath caught.

"I'm tired," he said, "of not letting myself fall in love."

She didn't say anything for a long time. "They're idiots," she finally said. "Complete idiots, the lot of them."

"No," he replied. "They aren't. I don't tend to hold idiots in affection."

"No?"

"Of course not," he said. "Why do you think I like you best of everyone?"

She didn't say anything. He could see the clouds coming closer now, dark swells creeping across the sky.

"I am not outrageous." Her voice was small. "I don't wish to be outrageous."

"I know," he said. "And I've forgotten how to be anything but the most flagrantly outrageous man ever."

She drew in a breath. "This was supposed to be the last time I saw you."

"It's the only sensible thing to do. We sound like the most ridiculous match; I know we do. But I can't help but think, Rose, that if we could get over this awkward beginning bit—if we could just get to the part where you tell me about mathematics over breakfast and I buy you telescopes and we spend half the evening kissing—"

She made an annoyed noise.

"Too much? A quarter of the evening kissing?" he amended.

"No." She straightened from the telescope. "The sun's gone behind the clouds." She glanced at him. "We've lost it for now. Maybe the weather will clear up." She glared out over the city.

He didn't put the chances high. The clouds had gone even darker; they stretched as far as he could see. She rubbed her gloved hands together briskly, and he realized that she was almost certainly cold.

He was, too—his hands and feet were uncomfortably chilled. He just hadn't noticed, because...he'd been watching her. Hell, he'd been spilling his heart out to her, such as he did these things. He'd just told her he hoped to marry her, and he wasn't even sure if she had noticed.

"An eighth of the evening kissing?" He looked over at her. "I can go lower if necessary."

She shut her eyes. "Stephen." That single word, long and drawn out. It was neither yes nor no; he wasn't sure what it was.

"Every time I'm with you," she said, "I tell myself I must beware. That this is what you do—make women comfortable, make us forget ourselves, principle by principle." She rubbed her forehead and slowly opened her eyes.

The light in the spire was waning even as she spoke, and yet for some reason, it seemed to find her, glinting in her eyes, reflecting off the warm brown of her skin. It caught a faint tilted smile on her mouth.

"So why is it," she said, "that I have just now noticed that you've only ever come to me about me? You've asked about my work, my thoughts, my wants. You set this up for me, and when I balked, you handed me the keys and walked away. If you wanted me to forget myself, you wouldn't keep reminding me of who I am."

"Rose, love," he said in a low voice, "I think you know why that is."

She inhaled and spread her hands against her belly. Then, very slowly, she walked closer to him—close enough that her skirts touched his trousers, close enough that he could have drawn her to him. She swallowed; he could have set his fingers against the hollow of her throat and felt the movement, so close was she.

She looked up into his eyes. "I don't want to dream timid dreams." Her voice was soft, with just a hint of a catch in it. "I want to dream large, vivid ones. I want to dream that you'll fall in love with me. That..." She bit her lip, but continued on. "That I could dare to reach out to you, that I needn't fear what would come."

She lifted her hand tentatively. He had thought that she might brush his cheek. But she didn't. Instead, she took his hand. They were both wearing gloves; he should not have felt a thrill at the brush of cloth on cloth. But he did, and it swept him from head down to toe, settling particularly in his groin, warming him in the cold air.

"But I do fear." Her hand clasped his. "You're clever and never off balance around others. You're handsome and sweet and outrageous. You could hurt me so badly, and I'm afraid to let you do it."

He swept his thumb along the side of her hand. "Sweetheart, if you don't trust me yet, there's no assurance I can give you that will put your mind at ease. All I can do is keep on not hurting you, and keep on, until you know in your bones I never will."

Their fingers intertwined, their hands coming together, palm to palm. He was enchanted, enraptured. She let out a long slow breath and slowly reached out with her other hand. This one she set on his shoulder. His skin prickled through his coat, his whole body tensing with her nearness. She drew a finger down his collarbone and then laid her palm flat against his chest.

He couldn't move.

"I trust you." Her voice was low, so low. "God knows I shouldn't—but I trust you."

She stepped even closer, skimming her hand down his arm, his elbow, and then bringing it back up to his shoulder. She took another step in, now, bringing her body even closer to his, warming the channel of air between them. He could feel the heat of her breath, the tension in her hand against his chest.

"Truthfully?" Stephen leaned down to whisper in her ear. "I can't pretend I'm fit for a decent woman—but if the question is whether I'll hurt you? No, Rose. Never. I adore you."

She took another step in, ducking her head as she did so, as if she did not want to look into his eyes. But her hand slid around his shoulder, drawing him full-length against her body.

Cold? It wasn't cold in the spire. How silly of him to think it had been. The air seemed almost hot around them. His whole body was coming to life with her against him. He put his arm around her—it seemed fair game, as she was pressing against him, and it was either that or hold it out awkwardly to the side. But she didn't protest at all. Instead, she set her forehead against his chest. Her hand slid down his back; his arm came around her shoulder.

She lifted her head. They were both breathing heavily.

"I don't think I should have touched you," she said shakily. "It's—it's..."

"It's nice." His own voice came out like gravel.

"It's too nice."

"It gets nicer."

She leaned against him. "How is that even possible?"

"Ah, well. I promised not to importune you, or you'd discover it. If I hadn't, this might be a little less chaste."

"Chaste?" She let out a shaky breath. "This isn't chaste. It's utterly wanton."

"On a scale of wantonness that ranges from..." He paused, trying to think of a suitable analogy. "From multiplication to astronomical parallaxes," he said, "embracing someone you care about while fully clothed ranks at about the arctangent level."

"Oh, dear. And I'm already so overheated."

A wave of his own heat washed over him at that, and he groaned, pulling her closer. "God, sweetheart. You're killing me."

She reached up tentatively, and set her fingers against his cheek. He stilled.

"May I slay you further?" she whispered.

"By all means," he replied, unable to move. "Kill me now."

His breath stopped. He couldn't do anything but watch her. She stood in place, her hands on him unmoving, as if gathering up the courage to move forward. Then slowly, very slowly, she came up on her toes. Her weight shifted; he could feel her hand against his jaw, her other hand against his chest, pressing all the harder.

Then her lips brushed his. She was kissing him—lightly at first, just sliding her lips against his, then pressing with greater firmness. He set his hand against the base of her spine and kissed her back.

There was nothing else, nothing but her, the weight of her in his arms, the warmth of her breath, the softness of her mouth.

"Rose," he said against her lips. "God, Rose." He shifted so that he could gather her up, so that the curves of her body slid against him.

She must have been able to feel his erection pressing against her, must have felt the tension in his arms as he held her close.

Usually at this point for Stephen, matters would have easily, swiftly progressed beyond a mere chaste close-mouthed kiss. But he'd promised Rose not to importune her—and no matter how urgently his body responded, there was something delicious about the slowness of the pace. He reveled in the sure knowledge that this would not be the last and only time he tasted her. He could slow everything down, enjoy the electric build-up of desire, delight in every gasp she gave.

"Have I earned a quarter of your evening yet, Miss Sweetly?" he murmured against her lips.

"I don't know." Her voice still had a quaver. "I need a little time to decide."

She kissed him again. He could have fallen into a trance, kissing her. Feeling her lips against his, awakening her first ardor with brush after brush of the lips. He wasn't sure when the kiss deepened, when he began taking her lips in his, when he first slid his tongue along her bottom lip. She responded with all the enthusiasm he'd ever hoped for, her tongue meeting his, tentatively at first, and then more boldly. He was lost in the feel of her. The space was close about them, warming to the point that the nearest window fogged over with condensation.

He wiped it clean, verified the clouds were still out in force—and then began kissing her again.

At some point, he simply lost his mind. Her hands had begun to roam and his had, too, cupping her breasts—which fit, so nicely rounded, in his palm. A kiss was one thing; running his thumb along the neckline of her gown, undoing buttons halfway down her bosom, sliding it down and then leaning over and nibbling... That was another thing entirely. A lovely, delicious, wonderful thing. She tasted faintly sweet.

Maybe that was his imagination. Maybe he only thought so because she was making the most captivating noises, little moans in the back of her throat halfway to purrs. He let his other hand drift down, cupping the juncture of her thighs over her skirts.

She made no noise of protest, not when he pushed harder, not when he pressed the ball of his hand against her, rubbing in a slow circle. He took his time about it, easing off and then coming back harder, pulling away and then returning, until she was almost as desperate as he was, until her hips were pressing against his hand, until she came apart against him. He felt her orgasm shudder through her, her limbs trembling. It was an almost electric sensation for him, too, watching her eyes flutter shut, watching her give herself up to him.

Her breath slowed after. She opened her eyes, looked up at him.

"Half the evening, do you think?" He gave her a long, slow smile.

That was when he realized that darkness had fallen while they'd been kissing. From the window, he could see a few beginning flurries falling to the ground, scarcely visible in the lamplight from the street below. He had no idea how long they'd been engaged in such pleasantries.

"Rose?" he said. "Are you…?" But he didn't know what to say beyond that. *Are you in love with me?* seemed too soon. The other words he burned to say—*touch me here, do that to me*—were too brazen. She was still dazed, unsure of herself, and slightly unsteady on her feet.

She still hadn't said anything.

"Right, then." He touched his thumb to her forehead, sliding it down the bridge of her nose. "Well. That settles that."

"Settles what?" They were the first words she'd spoken in God knew how long. He couldn't decipher the tone of her voice.

"We need more astronomical events," he said. "Because I am not waiting until the year 2004 to do this again."

Chapter Six

HE KNEW IT WAS A MISTAKE as soon as the words were out of his mouth. As soon as he heard himself and realized that it sounded like an invitation to tryst with him, rather than an offer to spend her life with him. She straightened, pulling away from him.

"Rose." He reached for her.

She brushed his hand away. "Don't. Please don't."

"Rose. I'm sorry. It was a joke."

"I know it was a joke." Her voice shook. "Of course it was a joke. It's always a joke to you."

She grabbed her cloak from the floor, found her gloves in the growing darkness.

"Rose."

Had he not been able to decipher her voice before? He'd not been listening hard enough. Now, now that he'd opened his mouth a moment too soon and spoken just a little too much… Now, he could hear the hurt in her tone.

"Rose. Sweetheart. I never meant to hurt you. You know that. You must know that."

She pulled on her gloves. "I know that. Stephen, I…" Her voice dropped. "You must know how I feel about you. But I don't think you understand. This isn't easy for me, and you aren't making it any easier. I want to trust you. I am trying to trust you. I even trust your intentions." Her voice dropped. "I don't trust your results."

"Rose."

She shook her head. "It's late. I promised my sister I'd be home just after four, and who knows now what time it is. I have to go."

"Rose."

"Thank you." She swallowed. "For bringing me here and arranging for a telescope."

"At least let me accompany you—"

"I think you've spent enough time with me at the moment. Please, Stephen. I told myself I wouldn't—and look at me. I need to think."

He rocked back, feeling as if he'd been punched. But he bit back his sharp reply. He'd hurt her first, after all. He'd talk to her when the sting of his ill-timed words had died down, when he was feeling more like himself— less vulnerable and more in control.

She swung down the ladder. He could scarcely see her descending into the gloom.

"Be careful," he called after her in a low voice.

She didn't say anything in response, not for a long while. But he heard her reach the top of the turret. She didn't move for a long time. He wondered if she was looking up at him, if she could see him in the gathering darkness. He wondered what she was thinking.

"I should have been careful hours ago," she said. "It's rather late for that."

⌘ ⌘ ⌘

THE HOUSE WAS NOT DARK when Rose returned; the lamps on the bottom floor were all lit. Rose could see a silhouette moving against the front window.

She thought back uneasily to the last toll of the clock. It was now…who knew how long after six?

The door was not locked. Her stomach hurt as she turned the handle, but it swung open on easy hinges and she walked into the light.

"*Now.*"Patricia's voice was hoarse and ragged.

It took Rose a moment, standing there blinking in the blinding light, to understand that her sister was not talking to her. Patricia sat on the sofa in a robe. Her hands were on her knees; she grimaced as she spoke, her whole body tensing.

Doctor Chillingsworth sat on a chair before her, looking at a watch.

Rose could see the tension in her sister's face, the grit of her teeth, the faint sheen of sweat at her temples. Rose stood in place, unsure of what she was observing.

The doctor, however, raised an unimpressed eyebrow. "Really, Mrs. Wells," he said reprovingly. "Do you really think that you can falsify a contraction and convince me?"

Patricia's hands gripped her knees. "Falsify? I wouldn't lie about such a thing."

Chillingsworth met this with a wave of his hand. "Exaggerate, then. The too-prominent grinding of teeth, the low noise in your throat—Mrs. Wells, you are a doctor's wife. It does not behoove you to behave in this fashion." Chillingsworth stood. "There is no cervical dilation; the, ah, *contractions*, as you call them, do not seem particularly intense. And the baby still has not turned. You've at least three weeks remaining by my estimation. This is false labor once again, Mrs. Wells. Try to sleep, and do make an effort not to bother me with trivialities until it is truly your time."

Patricia's face was a mask. Rose stepped forward, all the heat rising to her face. "Doctor Chillingsworth, my sister does *not*—"

Patricia interrupted this defense with a swift shake of her head. "Thank you for seeing me, doctor. I'm much obliged to you for putting my fears to rest. Now that you've explained what I must look for, I shall be sure not to bother you again until it is time."

"See that you don't." Chillingsworth ran a hand through his hair and glanced at his pocket watch once more. "Right in the middle of dinner," he muttered. He dropped the gold disc into his waistcoat pocket and gathered up his bag.

Patricia did not say anything until after he had left. For that matter, she didn't say anything immediately then. She simply sat on the sofa looking at Rose, while Rose stood in place, afraid to speak.

"I've been frantic," Patricia finally said. "Waiting for you to come home. I was afraid something had happened to you. I looked all over—up and down—I went to the Observatory myself, and they told me you weren't there. I was so frantic, and then I thought my contractions were starting."

It didn't matter what Stephen's intentions were. It didn't matter what he wanted. It didn't matter how sweet or how gentle he had been. It didn't even matter how much she loved him, how much she still yearned to run back to the spire and fall into his arms.

He hadn't made her forget herself; she'd just forgotten her sister.

Rose came in and sat on the chair Chillingsworth had vacated. "I'm so sorry, Patricia. But the transit of Venus…"

"Would not have been visible after sunset," Patricia said. "Or with the clouds that rolled in. I *do* listen to you. What were you doing?"

"I know it looks bad, but—"

"It *is* bad. I'm responsible for you, and you disappeared out from under my nose. Being out past sunset—that does not look good, Rose. Please tell me that you were with Dr. and Mrs. Barnstable the whole time, celebrating…whatever it is that astronomers celebrate."

Rose swallowed. "Um."

"Please tell me that Mr. Shaughnessy was not with you."

Oh, she could see it now. Patricia was right. It didn't just *look* bad. It was bad. What was she to do, lie to her sister for the rest of her life? Tell her she was marrying a man who would carry on in such a fashion? Their father had scraped and worked so hard to achieve even the barest measure of gentility. Was she to give it up so easily?

Rose examined her knuckles. "Did I..." She swallowed. "Did I not mention that I've been tutoring him in the methods of calculating astronomical distances?"

Patricia's eyes grew wide. "No. You know very well you did not mention any such thing."

"He may have set up a telescope in the church spire. So I could observe the transit."

"Together?"

Rose nodded.

"Alone?"

Another nod. Rose felt her cheeks burn in mortification.

"Did he hurt you?" Patricia demanded.

"No. He wouldn't." Not the way Patricia meant it anyway. "And don't look at me like that—I don't know what you must think of him, but he wouldn't hurt me." He would tell her that she was beautiful and brilliant. He would say that he liked her. But in the end, it would always come down to this—that if anyone found out that he was pursuing her, they would instantly think the worst.

"Oh, Rose. What am I to do with you?"

"How should I know?" Rose asked bitterly. "*I* don't know what to do with me, either."

Patricia didn't hesitate. She held out her hands. Rose stood, going to her, wrapping her arms around her.

"Sometimes," Rose said, "I can make myself remember that we live in two different worlds—he in his, and me in mine. Other times, I think that we live in the same place—one world, so much better because he's in it. I think I could fall in love with him, if only I dared." She swallowed. "But I can only dare to do so many things at a time." Her voice was thick. "And now, daring to do this one... I left you."

"Oh, Rose. You mustn't worry about me."

So like Patricia, to insist she needed nothing for herself.

"How can I not? I promised Doctor Wells I'd be here for you, and I wasn't."

"Shh. You're here now. And I do understand. Hypothetically speaking, I might have been willing to sneak out at night to see Isaac, when I was your age."

Rose smiled wanly. "Why, Patricia. We *are* speaking hypothetically, are we?"

"Oh, shh. Then say it's realistically speaking, too. Just…don't meet a man alone at night unless you're sure he'll marry you."

Rose sighed.

"And, ah, even then… Don't let things go too far."

"Whatever do you mean by that?" Rose asked innocently.

Too innocently, apparently, because Patricia gave her shoulder a slap. "Hussy. You're not that naïve. If you feel like falling asleep afterward, you've done too much."

"Oh, dear. I feel like falling asleep now," Rose told her, shutting her eyes.

"Cuddling with your sister doesn't count," Patricia said severely. "*I* don't have designs on your virtue. All I ever want to do at this point is sleep. Use the chamber pot and sleep."

"How indelicate."

"Anyone who thinks that ladies are delicate has either never been pregnant or has put the experience from her mind out of sheer horror."

Rose snorted. For a long while, they did not say anything. Rose held her sister's hands, her head resting against her shoulder. She could almost pretend that they were still young, that she was a child and Patricia not much older, that she was once again falling asleep to the sound of her sister's heartbeat.

But they weren't. Rose was twenty. Her sister was pregnant, and she had to take care of her. She had not thought anything would ever make her forget that…but then she'd underestimated Stephen Shaughnessy for too long.

He made her think this would all be easy—that all she had to do was love him and then all her problems would disappear. They wouldn't, though. They would multiply: his problems with hers. All he could do was what he'd managed tonight: He could make Rose forget herself long enough for real danger to threaten.

Rose buried her head in her sister's shoulder. "I'm sorry," she said. "I'll never leave you to worry like that again. I promise."

"I know."

After a long while, Patricia's hands squeezed her shoulders—not hard, but long—five seconds, then ten. Rose turned and looked at her. Her sister's breath came ragged; her jaw squared. Eventually, though, Patricia relaxed and glanced at the clock. "Forty-seven minutes," she said calmly. "They were forty-seven minutes apart."

"You had another contraction?" Rose sat up even straighter. "We should go get—"

Patricia shook her head. "False contractions, remember? Doctor Chillingsworth was just here."

"But—"

"Even if they are real," Patricia said, "which I doubt—they're still forty-seven minutes apart. They'll have to come much faster before it's time. We can fetch him then."

Chapter Seven

ROSE HAD EXPECTED TO SEE Mr. Shaughnessy on her walk into the observatory the next morning, but she did not encounter him. She wondered all day if he might come by, asking for another lesson—an excuse, of course, but she'd not have expected him to balk at inventing an excuse to see her—but every time the door opened, it was not him.

She was beginning to think that her worst fears had been right—that all he'd ever intended was a seduction, that he'd never wanted anything more—when she encountered him on her way home. She saw him, his scarf flapping in the wind, his hands in his pockets. He paced along the pavement, his face solemn. She did not know what to say to him.

He caught sight of her and gave a little shake of his head—not denial; by the tension that seemed to leave him, it rather looked like relief.

He came up to her. "Rose." His voice was low. "Before you send me on my way, let me be as clear as I can be. I love you. I have loved you for months, and I don't wish to do without you. I want to marry you. I want to buy you telescopes. I want you to have my babies. I want you, Rose. You and only you."

Oh, how it hurt to hear those words. She had suspected they must be true, even if part of her hadn't been able to make herself believe it.

"I love you," he said. "I didn't say it directly last night, and I ought to have. I love you. Marry me."

"Listen to you." She gave him a sad smile. "Have you given any thought at all to what this would mean? Given your reputation, it will be a terrible scandal if—when—you marry. Everyone will assume the worst of me."

"At first. It will blow over, though," he said confidently.

"Stephen. *Think.* Have you considered what it would mean for us to have children together?"

His eyes softened. "At length."

"No, you beast. I don't mean the begetting of them. Have you thought about what it would mean to have black, Irish, Catholic children?"

He blinked, slowly, and frowned. He really hadn't thought about it.

"You told me the awkward, difficult bit will only be the beginning," she said. "But it won't be. It'll be difficult in the middle, over and over. It'll be difficult at the end. It will never *stop* being difficult, and the only reason you don't know that is that you haven't considered the possibility. At some point, Stephen, you'll realize this is not a joking matter."

He spread his hands. "Maybe. But I'm not a worrier, Rose. It's not in my nature to fret about the future. Things happen as they do."

"Yes, and four years in, you'll realize what you've landed yourself in. You'll discover that it's not all kisses and telescopes. I give you credit for good intentions, Mr. Shaughnessy—but I don't think you're serious."

He spread his hands. "I'm not grave and sober, Rose. But I *am* serious about you. I know who I am and how I feel—and I'm not going to walk away from you simply because things may prove difficult. I don't worry about the future not because I'm blind to it, but because I don't see the point."

"Don't see the point! How can you want me if you don't even bother to think about what marriage to me would entail?" Her hands were shaking. "How can you say you love me and want to marry me, when you haven't even considered what that would mean?"

"At least I've said it," he snapped. "You haven't said what you mean at all, and I wish that you would. It's not that you think it will prove too difficult for *me*. You think it will be too difficult for *you*."

"My life is going to be difficult no matter who I marry." She raised her chin. "That's why I need to find someone who takes it seriously."

He leaned down to her. "There. Now you're saying what you mean. Finally. If you want a man who takes things seriously, you don't want me."

She opened her mouth to deny it…and then shut it. Her heart was breaking. She *did* want him. She wanted his laughter, his terrible jokes about mathematics. She wanted him handing her the key to the spire and telling her to go up alone. She wanted his practiced hands on her, coaxing her, seducing her, while he murmured in her ear. She wanted everything about him except…him.

"You don't make me forget myself." She shut her eyes. "But you make me forget who I have to be. You don't need an anvil, Stephen. You *are* the anvil. And you're right; I can't marry you."

His lips thinned. He looked at her, his eyes wild and fierce. And then he turned his head away and shrugged. "So be it. I'm an amusing fellow with no hidden depths. There's always some reason why I'm not suitable. I won't fret over it." He straightened, casting her a look. "I never do."

"Stephen…"

He shook his head. "Tell me if you change your mind, Rose. I won't alter mine. I may be frivolous—but I'm not faithless, and I'm not fickle."

"Stephen."

She didn't know what to say beyond that. She reached out and took his hand in hers. She couldn't bring herself to say words, didn't know what she could say even so. She just squeezed his fingers, not wanting to let go. Not being able to hold on.

"Be careful, Rose," he said with a nod of his head. And then he was drawing his hand away.

His thumb brushed hers briefly—but it was as temporary a warmth as his presence in her life. He smiled at her. "If you see me about," he said, "do talk Sweetly to me." And on that, he touched his hat and left.

⌘ ⌘ ⌘

ROSE SHUT THE DOOR behind her. Her hands were shaking; she felt sick to her stomach. But she had done it. She'd cut ties with Stephen Shaughnessy— and she'd survived it. She looked about the entry and frowned.

The house was dark. The sun had not yet set, but it was close enough to evening that a few lights ought to have been on. There were no lights in the front room, the dining room, the back pantry.

She frowned and tentatively called out. "Patricia?"

A door opened upstairs. A few moments later, Mrs. Josephs put her head over the railing.

"Your sister is not feeling so well, Miss Sweetly."

Rose frowned. "Has she seen the doctor?"

"Not since last night," the older woman said. "She says it's just more of that false labor again. She doesn't want to bother him."

Rose felt a pit of foreboding open in her stomach. "Didn't he say that false labor pains are supposed to stop? How can she be sure that it's false labor, and not something else?"

Mrs. Josephs shook her head. "I've never been blessed with a child, Miss. Really, I don't know a thing about it."

Rose shook her head and then carefully ascended the stairs. Her sister's room was dark, but Patricia was not in bed. She was walking a figure eight pattern on the carpet.

"Rose." Patricia looked up as her door opened. "You're back. Don't worry about me; I'll feel well soon enough. In fact, I don't feel so badly now." She managed a creditable smile.

"Should you lie down?"

"I feel better walking."

"What's wrong?"

"Nothing really," Patricia said. "Just more of those false labor pains, that's all. And they're not coming particularly swiftly—they're still only twenty-three minutes apart."

Rose felt cold fingers clutch her heart. "You're still having labor pains? They've gone on all day? They're coming closer together?"

"*False* labor pains." But Patricia sounded as if she were trying to convince herself. "It's too early for real labor. I...sent over another note to Doctor Chillingsworth at noon, and he replied that I had nothing to worry about from my description, that the only thing I needed to do was calm myself."

"I do not like Doctor Chillingsworth," Rose said passionately.

"He makes me a little uneasy, too," Patricia said, far too nicely as always. "But I don't want to bother him with a triviality. If I do, maybe he'll not come when it's urgent. So for now..." Patricia smiled. "He's only five minutes away, less if Josephs runs. It's doing me no harm to wait. And if I'd rather walk, it can't be that bad, can it?"

No need to frighten her sister, no matter how Rose's heart pounded or what scenarios her imagination invented. "No, of course not," Rose said. "You'll feel better tomorrow, no doubt. For now, do you want me to walk with you?"

"Yes. That would be lovely."

Rose took her sister's hand and paced with her along that four-foot strip of carpet. Patricia's steps were slow and hesitant, but her voice was as welcoming as ever.

"Did you have a good day today?"

Rose hesitated. She could talk about her calculations, about the story Mrs. Barnstable had told her. But Patricia would see through her false humor in a moment. She was already peering at Rose, a frown on her face.

"I told Mr. Shaughnessy I couldn't see him any longer," Rose said swiftly.

"Oh, Rose. I know you had to do it—but I'm sorry you did."

Rose shook her head. "It's for the best, really. But..."

"But you liked him anyway, even though he's a rake."

"But I wish I were someone else," Rose heard herself say instead. "Someone who didn't have to think so hard about marrying an outrageous fellow without risking anything."

"Marry?" Patricia turned her head to look at Rose. "He wasn't talking marriage, was he?"

They made another circuit of the carpet, her feet falling on flowers, before Rose felt ready to respond. "He was," Rose said softly.

"Did you doubt his future fidelity?"

Oh, she should have. All of England would doubt his future fidelity—all of it but her.

"No," Rose said, her voice on the verge of breaking. "No, not that. But I'd be in all the gossip papers. They'd sneer at Papa for being in trade. And that would be only the beginning. It would be hard. Every day would be hard, and he simply won't admit how hard it would be."

"Oh, Rose." Patricia's hand clenched in hers. "I love you. But sometimes you have to do what you most want in life. You can't hide from everything."

"I don't *hide,*" Rose said, stung.

Patricia didn't speak for a moment.

Rose thought of her portfolios, her columns of numbers. She thought of the transit of Venus, of her ducking her head and insisting she'd never be attached to a scientific voyage.

It's not that you think it'll prove too difficult for me. *It will be too difficult for* you.

"I don't hide," she said, more slowly this time.

"You do. A little. And you have ever since you were small. It's why Papa broke with Grandpapa all those years ago, you know."

"What?"

"When Papa moved to London from Liverpool? It wasn't just to set up that first import store. It was because he didn't like what Grandfather was doing to you—putting you on display, having you do your little adding trick with the basket in front of the crowds. You *weren't* shy before then. After that… Papa wanted it to stop, but Grandfather said it brought in customers." Patricia shrugged. "So Papa and Mama left instead."

Rose swallowed. She hadn't realized they'd left for her. She had thought… Well, she'd been too young to think of reasons. She had simply thought that her parents wanted to strike out on their own.

All she could remember when they moved was a feeling of gladness— that she could stop feeling ashamed of the best part of herself, that she could sit and revel in her talent without everyone's eyes on her. She had stopped belonging to other people.

She had always thought it a happy accident. It hadn't been; it had been a gift from her parents.

"So I worry about you sometimes." Patricia squeezed her hand. "I worry about you a lot, in fact, ensconcing yourself in a quiet office with nothing but numbers to keep you company."

"It's not just numbers," Rose said. "I like astronomy. It's exciting. And it feels so…safe. Nothing else is about for millions of miles."

But she hadn't felt alone last night. Last night, when she'd taken his hand and kissed him, she had felt brave. Not afraid that the world would laugh at her, not with him at her side.

Patricia squeezed her hand again—but this time in a hard, lengthy clench. It was only because she stopped walking that Rose realized she didn't intend it as a comforting gesture; she was having another contraction.

"Patricia," Rose said, when she finally loosened her grip, "I really think we should send for Chillingsworth."

Chapter Eight

ROSE HELD HER BREATH as Doctor Chillingsworth frowned. It had taken Josephs hours to find him; he'd been with another patient when Josephs had first set out. The doctor had come only reluctantly; he seemed tired now, his left eyelid drooping asymmetrically.

He'd turned the lights on full bore and felt Patricia's belly with a clinical detachment.

"Thirty-seven weeks along," he said with a shake of his head. "Thirty-seven weeks, if that. The baby's not yet turned. There's no dilation to speak of. Mrs. Wells, it is still not your time."

At least he was actually addressing Patricia now. Not that he had any choice; Mr. Josephs had not come up to the bedroom.

"But I'm having contractions," Patricia said. "Regular contractions, coming closer and closer together. The time between them has fallen from forty-five minutes last night to nineteen just now."

Chillingsworth looked at Patricia. He let out a long, long sigh. "And yet you are...*mistaken*, I suppose I shall say charitably. There are a great many changes that occur in the human body during a period of gravidity. No doubt you are experiencing gas."

"Gas." Patricia sounded shocked. "No. It's not gas."

"Your husband is absent," Chillingsworth said, "And no doubt you find yourself in want of attention. I have observed it all too often in women in your state. But you are worrying yourself needlessly and no doubt causing more harm than not. Rest assured that it is not your time. I do not need more dramatics from you." He shook his head. "I'd have a little more patience with a new mother's antics—but I was called here at eleven in the evening after an exceedingly taxing day. Please show some consideration for others, Mrs. Wells."

He packed up his things. Patricia's lips had thinned considerably; her hands clenched together. She didn't speak a word, and Rose couldn't blame her.

Dramatic? In want of attention? *Her* sister? There was not a chance in the world of it. Patricia had never done a thing to draw attention to herself.

Rose wanted to talk to the man sharply.

But Patricia simply said, "Yes, Doctor Chillingsworth. I'm sorry to have disturbed you."

If Patricia didn't want to make a fuss, Rose wouldn't make one for her. After all, wasn't that the way of the world? Rose rarely made a fuss for herself; it was seeing the people she loved be treated unfairly that made her angry.

Rose sat with her sister long after Chillingsworth had left, holding Patricia's hand, not saying a word, trying not to count the minutes that elapsed between squeezes.

She fell asleep in her clothes, trying to convince herself that the squeezes were not coming closer and closer together.

⌘ ⌘ ⌘

SHE WOKE IN THE DARK, disoriented and bewildered.

"Rose." Patricia was shaking her. Her voice was a little ragged. "Rose, my water just broke."

"Oh my God." Rose came out of her confused dreams instantly. "Oh, God. I'll wake Josephs. He can have Chillingsworth here in ten minutes."

"Yes," Patricia said. "Yes. I think that's for the best now."

Rose ran down stairs. She knocked sharply on the servants' door and explained the situation. In no time, Josephs was stomping into his boots and setting off. Rose watched him go out the door into a wild flurry of snow.

A bell tower chimed twice in the darkness; Rose closed the door and ascended the stairs to her sister.

"He'll be here soon," she said. "Mrs. Josephs is fetching towels and putting water on to boil."

She fumbled with a spill, igniting the rolled paper from the coals before lighting the lamp.

Patricia had her hands on her belly. "This is happening." She gave Rose a wan smile. "This is actually happening. How…exciting."

Exciting, Rose suspected, was not her first choice of word. Nor her second.

"Very exciting."

Rose didn't say the other thing on her mind—that at thirty-seven weeks, it was too soon. What happened would happen; if Patricia didn't want to fret,

Rose would keep her worries to herself. It would all be well. It would be. And Chillingsworth would be here soon.

"I wish Isaac were here," Patricia said.

So did Rose, and not just because Patricia's husband was a doctor.

"Don't you worry," Rose said. "I'll make sure you're taken care of. I promised."

Five minutes passed, then ten. Patricia's contractions were coming closer now—mere minutes apart, and from the strain on her face, they were getting worse. Fifteen minutes had elapsed since Josephs left, when a third contraction came. Patricia gritted her teeth; Rose held her shoulders. "Shh, shh," she whispered. "It will all be well."

But even after the contraction passed, Patricia remained as she had been, her teeth set, her breathing ragged.

"There, there," Rose said soothingly. "You're doing so well."

Patricia's hand slipped to her belly once more. "Rose?"

"Yes?"

"I've just thought of something."

Rose set her hand on her sister's shoulder. "What is it? I'll make it better."

Patricia let out a shaky breath. "The baby hasn't turned yet."

Rose stared at her sister in horror. For one moment, she couldn't find any words of comfort at all. Every snatch of remembered conversation, every story she'd heard of what might happen in labor floated to mind.

She caught herself before she could recoil in horror. "You mustn't worry," she said. "Chillingsworth will be here soon. We live in modern times. There's a great deal that can be done. I'm sure of it. Don't you worry."

As she spoke, the door opened below.

It was a sign of how frightened she was that the thought of Chillingsworth—self-important, cold, rude Chillingsworth—warmed her through and through. "There," she said soothingly. "He's here now. I imagine he was only delayed because of the snow."

There was some stomping in the entry, followed by footsteps coming up the stairs. "You see?" Rose told her sister. "It will be…"

The door swung open on the lonely form of Mr. Josephs. For a second, Rose waited, watching him in utter silence. It took her that second to understand that something was wrong—that the footsteps she'd heard just now had been solitary, that no doctor followed on his heels.

Mr. Josephs hung his head wearily. "He's not coming."

Rose blinked, trying to comprehend what had just been said. "He's out on another call?"

"No," Josephs said shortly. "He's in. He's just not coming."

Rose felt all her hope slowly drain from her.

Patricia pressed her hand. "What does that mean?"

Josephs shook his head. The thing he didn't say—well, Rose could hear it echoing all too well. Chillingsworth referring to her sister as "dramatic," saying that she was "mistaken" and thinking himself charitable for not calling her an outright liar.

Rose stood. "There's a misunderstanding," she said tightly. "A mistake. He just needs someone to explain what is happening to him." That had to be it. "We didn't tell Josephs your water broke. No doubt once he hears that, he'll be right over."

"No, Miss," Josephs started to say. "I told him—"

Rose held up a hand, stopping those words. She couldn't accept them. She'd promised Patricia that she would take care of her; she couldn't let her down. Not now. "I'm going," she said. "I'll get him. I'll be right back, Patricia. Right back. Mr. Josephs, have your wife come up and sit with my sister. You'll need to come with me."

It was a good thing Rose had fallen asleep in her clothing. She had only to find stockings and boots—no point doing them up all the way—and slip into her coat. She was winding a scarf about her neck when Mr. Josephs came down to her.

"Miss," he said in a low voice. "Perhaps you need to hear…"

"Don't say it." She couldn't hear it.

"Mrs. Walton, the midwife—she *is* out. That's why I was so long returning. I was checking on her. I can find someone else, but the next nearest physician is miles away, and in this snow…"

"Do *not* say it," Rose warned. "If the next nearest physician is miles away, then we will simply have to get Chillingsworth." She thought of her sister's face twisting in fear. Of her sister trying to be brave as she told her the baby hadn't turned. "We will *have* to get him."

The snow was falling in earnest; Rose could scarcely see more than two houses down. The street lamps were like dull white globes of light, scarcely illuminating their way. Three steps in the snow—now three inches deep—made Rose realize she should have taken the time to lace her boots. Snow slipped in, cold and wet, packing itself against her stockings with every step. But she didn't dare stop. She counted time not in minutes, but in the length of time between Patricia's contractions. She could almost feel the squeeze of her sister's hand in hers as she hurried down the street.

It took two contractions to arrive at Chillingsworth's home. She rapped smartly on the door. In her mind's eye, she could see her sister smiling gamely, trying to put a good face on things.

No, Rose told herself. It was going to be all right. She would make it all right.

The door finally opened. Chillingsworth's eyes fell on Rose; in the flickering light of the streetlamp outside, she could see his nostrils flare.

"Please," Rose said. "My sister's water broke. The baby is coming now. It hasn't turned—"

"Of course it hasn't turned," the doctor said in a cold voice. "It's not her time yet."

"No, it is. It is absolutely her time. She's laboring now, Doctor Chillingsworth, truly laboring. There can be no question—"

"And how many births have you presided over?"

"None, but—"

"Did you *see* her water break?"

"No, but our woman was cleaning—"

"Miss Sweetly, I spent ten years at a naval post in the West Indies. While I was there, I saw a hundred women like your sister, and let me tell you, a more dramatic set of lying malingerers I have never observed. I have gone to your sister twice in the last twenty-four hours. I will not rouse myself for her again."

"But—"

"I shall wait on Mrs. Wells at seven in the morning, which is far earlier than she deserves. No sooner. Tell your sister to stop with her hysterics and behave with some decency."

Rose was too shocked to speak.

"And for God's sake, if you bother me again tonight, I'll not come in the morning, either."

"Doctor Chillingsworth. Please."

He shut the door in her face.

"I tried to tell you, Miss." Beside her, Josephs sounded apologetic. "I did."

He had, and she hadn't wanted to listen. She hadn't *dared* to listen, because there was no one else to be found at this time of night but this man.

This man who had spent ten years in the West Indies. Who had called Patricia dramatic, had accused her of falsifying her condition simply because she craved attention.

I saw a hundred women like your sister, he had said. For weeks she'd listened to Chillingsworth talk. For weeks, she had wanted to believe that when he said *women like your sister* he had meant women who were pregnant with their first child. But he hadn't qualified his comments with a statement about pregnant women. He'd talked about working in the West Indies.

A more dramatic set of lying malingers I have never observed.

It was a punch to the stomach. Rose inhaled. The cold air felt like a knife in her lungs. But she didn't have time to weep over it or to gnash her teeth at the unfairness. She didn't have time to rail at life's injustices.

In the back of her mind, she was still counting contractions—and she knew now that they were coming even closer.

"Josephs." She was proud of herself; her voice was steady. "Find someone. Anyone. Please. I'm…"

She paused. Odd, how times like this made everything clear. There was no room for worry or second-guessing, no space for wounded pride any longer. There was nothing but her sister.

"I'm going to find someone who will help," she said.

Chapter Nine

SOMEONE WAS POUNDING on Stephen's door.

It was his first coherent thought upon waking—that hard, repeated tattoo beating in time with an urgency he did not understand, but felt instinctively in his blood.

He came out of bed, put on trousers and a loose shirt, and slipped downstairs.

He opened the door onto a white flurry of snow—and in dark counterpoint, with the streetlight behind her making a golden halo about her, Rose Sweetly. She had a cloak pulled about her, but her teeth were chattering noisily.

"Rose?" He had to be dreaming, but from experience, his dreams of her had never had her so bundled up.

"Stephen." She sounded almost frantic. "I don't know what to do. Patricia is in labor—her water broke—the baby's coming and it's still breech—"

"I'll go fetch someone."

"No." She turned her head away and swiped at her eyes. "Mrs. Walton is out on another call, and Doctor Chillingsworth is…not available. Josephs is off in search of someone farther afield, but there is no time. The baby is coming *now*, and I don't know what to do."

He'd never seen her so upset. Little crystals of ice clung to her eyelashes, to the corners of her eye. Frozen tears, he realized. Her lips quivered.

"Right," he heard himself say. "My father was a stable master. I've birthed dozens of horses, one of them breech. It's not the same thing—"

But she was on the verge of a panic, and she needed him.

"—but I'm happy to come," he finished. "Don't worry. It's going to be all right."

"That's what I kept telling Patricia." Her teeth chattered. "And it just keeps getting worse and worse instead."

"Well, you're going to have to keep telling your sister that," he said. "That's your job now, Rose. You keep telling her that—and we'll make sure it's true. Come along."

He found a pair of shoes in the hall.

"You're coming like that?"

"No point wasting time. You're only two houses down, after all."

Rose nodded. It was cold outside—cold enough for the wind to cut right through the linen of his shirt, cold enough to drive the last remnants of his weariness from him. He followed her to her home. When she fumbled with her key, he took it from her numb fingers, unlocking the door.

"Rose," he said as she took off her cloak in the hallway. "The most important thing is that you must not let her panic. You're her sister. It doesn't matter if there's reason for her to be frightened; we must do our best not to scare her. You're in command. I'm just here to make jokes. Understand?"

She paused looking up at him.

He set a finger on her chin. His hands were cold, but her skin was colder. No knowing how long she'd been outside looking for someone. Her lips parted; for a second, she looked up at him as if expecting a kiss. For a second, he wanted to give her one.

Instead, he took a handkerchief from his pocket and very gently wiped the ice crystals from her lashes.

"There," he said quietly. "That's better. You can do this."

She drew in a shuddering breath. He reached out and took her hand in his. Her fingers were deathly cold; he rubbed them between his palms.

"Come," she said. "Let's go."

As she ascended the stairs, her chin came up. Her jaw squared; he could see her gathering determination with every step.

She entered the room to the left of the small hallway.

"Patricia," she announced. "I've returned."

Stephen followed behind her. The room was warm and comfortable. A fire crackled on the hearth. Mrs. Wells was in bed, her head turned to the side. An older woman sat in a chair next to the bed, watching over her.

He'd only ever seen Mrs. Wells properly attired. Now she was in a loose-fitting gown. Her dark hair was held back by a kerchief. She took one long look at Stephen. "He's not a doctor," she said in a low tone.

"No," Rose said firmly. "Chillingsworth…was otherwise detained. Patricia, you know Mr. Shaughnessy."

"Mrs. Wells." Stephen nodded at her.

"Stephen Shaughnessy." A smile played along her lips. "Actual Man. My. I feel better already."

"Mr. Shaughnessy has presided over many births," Rose said in a commanding voice. "He'll make sure all goes well."

Stephen was not so sure about that, but he tried to look…well, competent.

Mrs. Wells raised an eyebrow at him. "Mr. Shaughnessy. I knew you were an Actual Man, but I had not thought you so…prolific."

"Not my children," he said.

"Oh." She contemplated this. "Not human, either, then, I take it."

"Horses."

"Well, then." Mrs. Wells swallowed. "Do we try to turn the baby?"

He regarded her thoughtfully. "I don't think we can," he said. "At this point in labor? I'm not sure it's possible, and if it is, none of us know how to do it."

"If there are any minor complications," Rose said, "Mr. Shaughnessy will see to it."

"And if there are major ones?" He could hear the strain in Mrs. Wells's voice.

"Then the birth will take a little longer," Rose said matter-of-factly, "and by the time greater expertise is needed, Josephs will have returned with another doctor."

"Yes," Stephen said. "So you're in good hands. The best hands, Mrs. Wells. Your body knows what to do; it is doing it as we speak. Don't fight it; do what your body tells you."

"But the baby is coming breech."

"Hundreds of babies are born breech every day," Stephen said. "Hundreds of babies the world over—many of them without complications or further incidents. It'll be a little harder on you, but you can manage."

It wasn't fast. Rose draped a sheet over her sister for modesty's sake as the contractions came closer and closer. Mrs. Wells began to cry out with every passing wave; when she tried to choke back her moans, Rose encouraged her.

"Yell if you must," Rose said. "You're letting the world know the baby is coming."

Stephen didn't know when he became the one to hold Mrs. Wells's hand. He didn't even know when the room began to lighten from the burnished gold illumination cast by the lamp to the pale gray of dawn. The hours blurred together.

"There you are," Rose said. "The feet are coming. Oh, Patricia. They're the most darling feet."

Mrs. Wells made a noise that might, under other circumstances have been a laugh.

"You're almost there," Stephen said. "You have it, Mrs. Wells."

She gritted her teeth again and let out another cry.

"Patricia, he's a boy."

"There you are," Stephen said. "All your friends will be jealous—they had to birth their babies all the way before they knew the sex. Here you are, beating them out."

Mrs. Wells did laugh at that. "Yes," she said with a shake of her head. "Surely they will all be jealous of my thirty-some hours of labor."

Another push; her hands dug into his arm, hard—but nothing. When her contraction subsided, she gritted her teeth.

"Next one," he told her.

But it wasn't—not that one, nor the one after that. Out the window, the sun had come out. The snow had stopped falling; a little light played on tree branches laden with a heavy white blanket.

Another push came, and it, too, was futile. Mrs. Well's face glistened with sweat; her jaw squared in determination.

"Rose." Stephen gestured. She looked up.

"You need to lend your sister a hand on the next push."

"What—how—should I pull?" She looked dubious.

"No. Have Mrs. Josephs take your place. Come here."

She stood.

"Set your hand here." He gestured to her abdomen. "Feel—you should be able to find the baby's head. A nice round lump. Yes?"

She nodded.

"Good. Then as soon as her next contraction comes, push. Start off gently; push harder and harder as she does, too."

"But—"

Stephen took hold of her free hand. "You can do it, Rose."

It came in the next instant. Mrs. Wells gritted her teeth and let out a moan. Rose squared her jaw and pushed. And then—just a moment later—they heard a low wail.

"Oh." Mrs. Wells's voice was hoarse and ragged. "Oh, thank God."

"He looks healthy." Mrs. Josephs sat at the edge of the bed. "Not that I'm an expert in babies—but he's moving and breathing and crying…"

"Let me have him." Patricia's voice was weak but triumphant.

Mrs. Josephs stood. She wrapped a white cotton towel around dark, glistening chestnut skin. A tiny hand pulled at the air; a foot kicked out. A minuscule face scrunched in protest.

Stephen was not a baby sort of person. They'd always seemed strange, clumsy things to dote over—human beings that were not yet old enough to be interesting.

But *this* baby might have been the most beautiful thing Stephen had ever seen. Every toe seemed perfectly formed. The whole room seemed bathed with light.

"Excellent work," he heard himself say. It seemed inadequate to the occasion.

Mrs. Wells took her child, holding him to her. Her eyes were shining. In fact, the entire world seemed to shimmer, and Stephen found himself surreptitiously wiping his own eyes.

Rose and her sister were holding each other, speaking in barely coherent sentences, and Stephen realized he was extraneous.

Scarcely a friend. Definitely not family. He'd only been the man who was close enough to help when no one else was around. He hadn't slept; his presence in a woman's bedchamber was entirely improper, and…and…

He stayed long enough to make certain that the cord was cut, the after birth properly expelled.

He wished he could stay longer, wished that he belonged here. But this wasn't the time to demand attention—not now, when the sisters were basking in victory after a hard-fought war. This moment was about everyone but himself.

He smiled at the two of them and then slowly, quietly slipped out of the room.

⌘ ⌘ ⌘

MRS. JOSEPHS HAD LEFT to fetch some hot water for her sister, who was doing her best to stay awake with little Isaac in her arms, when Rose realized that Stephen was no longer in the room. She absented herself swiftly, ran to the stairwell—and caught sight of him below, staring bemusedly at the door in the entry.

"Stephen," she called.

He turned around, tilting his head up. He looked every bit as exhausted as she felt. His shirt had long since lost any hint of crispness; it was unbuttoned past his throat, showing a triangle of pale skin and dark, wiry hairs.

"I'll be on my way shortly," he said with a small smile. "It's just that I've realized it's broad daylight—and it will be extraordinarily shocking if I'm seen walking out of your door. Particularly looking like this." His hand swept down.

She followed his gesture. His sleeves were rolled to his elbow, showing a shocking, delicious amount of skin. His trousers were wrinkled—which only made them mold to his thighs all the more. Without a coat, the linen of his shirt clung to his shoulders—and if she remembered the gossip correctly, hadn't he done some rowing at Cambridge? He looked like he had.

And she could see precisely what he meant. Bedroom slippers; shirtsleeves. It would be shocking indeed.

"Oh, dear." Rose found herself drifting down the stairs toward him. "Oh, dear. I see what you mean. If you go out like that, you'll start a veritable riot."

He blinked once…and then ever so slowly, he began to smile.

"You can't leave without letting me thank you."

"Ah, Rose. There's no need for that."

She descended the staircase. "There's every need. After what I told you yesterday—"

A sharp rap sounded on the door. Rose frowned—and then realized that Mrs. Josephs was assisting her sister upstairs and Mr. Josephs had not yet returned. She was the only one who could answer the door, and Stephen was standing right here, in a shocking state of undress. Not that she was doing much better; her gown was stained. It wasn't just wrinkled; it looked as if it had spent the last year wadded up in the back of the wardrobe.

"Go to the back room," she said to Stephen. "Quickly."

He winked at her and disappeared.

Rose smoothed her hands over her gown, which did nothing at all. The cause was hopeless, and so she gave up on it and opened the door anyway.

She really ought not to have been surprised at the man who stood there. He had, after all, promised to come in the morning. But at the sight of Doctor Chillingsworth, all the emotion she'd hidden over the course of the night bubbled to the surface—all her fear, her despair. Every last ounce of impossible worry that she had swallowed came back in one blinding rush.

"Doctor Chillingsworth," she said in a cold voice.

He looked down his nose at her. "I am here as promised."

"You are too late," she heard herself say. "Patricia gave birth an hour ago."

His face did not even flicker at this news. He didn't look surprised. He didn't apologize for his hateful words the previous night.

"Ah, did she?" he said instead.

She felt her hands clench into fists at her sides. "You said it wasn't her time." No. It wasn't despair that filled her. It was a cold fury, one that threatened to overwhelm her. "You said she was a *lying malingerer*—"

He shrugged. "Well, there was some chance I was mistaken—there is always that chance. But I figured there'd be no real harm. Women of her sort are like cows: They scarcely need any assistance when dropping their calves."

He stepped into the entry and took off his coat, oblivious—or perhaps just indifferent—to Rose's splutter.

"I suppose I'll take a look now."

Lying malingerer. Women of her sort are like cows. It was too much—far, far too much.

She took a step toward him. "When Doctor Wells left, he asked me to stand in his stead—to tell him every time I heard the baby's heartbeat, to convey every last kick I felt."

It had not been so long ago that she'd held her sister's hand, had put her hands on her sister's belly and pushed her son's head that last inch. They had not needed this man—but they might have. It staggered her what might have happened had things been even an iota worse. His absence could have meant the baby's life. Or Patricia's. And to him, this was a matter that he could shrug off. She could scarcely think for the anger that filled her.

"On behalf of my sister's husband," Rose said, "this is for you."

So saying, she punched him in the stomach. She felt the blow travel all the way up her arm, stinging in the most gratifying way. His breath blew out; he gave a satisfying grunt.

"This is for her." Rose punched him again. "And this is for *me.*" She made to ram her fist into his belly again, but he caught her wrist this time.

"Why, you little—"

"You'd better let go of her." The words came from behind her. Rose felt herself smile—a beautiful, impossible, gratifying smile.

Chillingsworth froze. He looked up at Stephen, who had come into the entry. "And you are?"

"Taller than you," Stephen said. "Stronger than you. Younger than you. And at this moment, I'm angrier than you, too. Let go of Miss Sweetly and get out of here before I hold you down for her to pummel."

The doctor released her wrist. He stepped back and then shakily took his coat from the hook.

"Get out, then," Stephen said.

He took another step forward; Chillingsworth wrenched open the door, letting in a blast of cold air, and then, as swiftly as he could, he vanished. The door slammed behind him.

Rose could hear her own breathing echoing wildly in the entry. She'd punched a man. Twice. And he'd deserved it.

And Stephen...

She turned to him. He was looking at her with the most intense expression on his face, one that made her whole body tingle from head to toe.

"Stephen." She took a step toward him. "Stephen."

He raised a finger and set it on her lips. "Don't promise anything when your emotions are running high," he said. "Or when you're exhausted."

Tired though she was, Rose had never felt more certain. All her fretting had burned away.

She didn't know when she'd become sure. Not when he'd sat with her sister. Not when he'd agreed to come with her. Maybe it was when Chillingsworth had sent her away, when Rose had not known where to turn…until she had known. She had known that help was not a million miles away, but right next door. That she had only to stretch out her hand and ask, and it would be hers.

She had known. She had gone to him, and he had come.

"Now," he said, "have you a coat I could borrow so that I could look respectable long enough to return home?"

She smiled up at him. "Of course. I have everything you need."

She found one of Isaac's old jackets and a pair of his boots in a trunk and brought them out. He was sitting on the sofa, looking somewhat dazed. He smiled at her wearily.

"Here," Rose said. "Let's get these on you."

They were both too large on Stephen's frame. He let Rose do up his buttons. Her hands trembled as she did. She'd kissed him, let him touch her. But somehow, this seemed the most intimate act yet, the sort of favor that wives performed for husbands.

When she'd done the last button, she looked up into his eyes. She'd expected, maybe, to see a reflection of her own emotion.

Instead, his gaze was hard and utterly unreadable.

"You're exhausted," she said. But that was not all it was.

"I'm contemplating." His words came slowly.

"Here. Let's get you home, where you can rest."

He didn't resist her tug on his arm. Rose put on her own coat, opened the door to the house, and glanced down the street. It was empty but for the drifts of snow.

"Quickly," she told him, "while nobody's about."

She accompanied him. Maybe she needed to make sure he arrived safely; maybe it was because he seemed strangely subdued, and she feared he'd not think properly. He unlocked his own door and then looked down at her.

"You were right," he said. "I didn't understand how difficult things might be for you—not until just now at the very end."

The fear she'd been trying not to feel washed through Rose. He'd stopped her from making a declaration. Of course he had; he'd seen what Chillingsworth had said and done, had understood all the indignities she'd face, small and large. And of course he'd changed his mind. She stared up at him, stricken.

"The Irish are accounted violent drunkards," he said. "Gamblers with no sense of responsibility, and terrible human beings, through and through. But at least we're considered human beings."

Rose would not let her heart break. Not here, not in the snow, not with her sister's new child next door. She would stand here and look him in the eyes. She would…

She choked and looked down.

"But there's something you don't understand," he said. "When I said I loved you, I didn't mean that I would walk away when I realized your life was difficult. The fact that I understand how hard things can be means that I want to stand by you sooner, and try even harder to make it better."

She could scarcely believe it. She lifted her face to his, her heart pounding.

And then he smiled at her, and all her fears took flight.

"I love you," he said. "Let me buy you telescopes and kiss you half the night. And when things grow difficult, let me be make them a little easier."

She looked up at him. She felt dazed, utterly worn out. And so she said the first thing that came to her mind, which happened to be…

"Did you know that Dr. Maro in Italy has calculated the likelihood that the earth will be struck by an asteroid at two hundred and fifty million to one?"

He blinked. "No. I did not know that. Is it…relevant?"

"Yes," she heard herself say. And then she reached out and opened his door, and before her nerve left her, she stepped inside.

He followed her, scratching his head in bemusement.

"Yes," she told him. "It's very relevant. You see, it's one hundred and sixty times more likely that the earth will be struck by an asteroid than that you will seduce me. And yet…" She swallowed, looking up at him. "I find myself seduced. Utterly. The only explanation is that we are all about to perish."

He looked down at her, his breath hissing out. "Rose. Darling."

"And since we are going to die anyway…" Her throat felt dry. "Would you…take me to bed?"

He looked at her. Really looked at her. His eyes were dark; a light danced in them. He leaned over her and drew one finger down her cheek.

"Rose," he said. "I have just one question."

She nodded.

"Does probability really work like that?"

Her cheeks burned and she ducked her head. "No," she moaned, feeling rather ashamed. "It doesn't. I'm sorry—I was going to tell you afterward. And I know that doing such a thing under false pretenses…" She let out a little laugh. "I know it doesn't make sense. But I love you, and…and… I think that if we are to do this, I must learn to be a little outrageous." She swallowed. "And in a few hours my parents will be here, and once we're engaged, it'll be four months before we'll be left alone, and—"

"Four months! No, never mind that for now. Rose, did you just lie to me about *mathematics* to get me into bed?" He laughed. "I don't think I've ever been so flattered." He took her hand. His fingers were warm against hers, and her whole body thrilled at his touch. "Come, Rose."

She followed him up the stairs.

His bed was solid wood, heaped with a quilt of shifting greens. He stopped on the threshold of his room. "Are you sure, Rose?"

Her heart was pounding. "I'm sure."

She wasn't sure what to expect. But he didn't pounce on her immediately. He didn't take off her clothing. Instead, he turned her to him, set his finger under her chin, and he kissed her.

It was a sweet, intense sort of kiss—soothing in it's own way. And yet his hand crept around her. His fingers touched the back of her neck. Her skin felt sensitive all over.

"Hullo, there, Rose," he murmured against her lips.

She smiled and tilted her head back. "Stephen. I love you."

"Ah, good."

His touch was gentle and yet so firm, caressing the base of her neck. She didn't even realize that he was undoing her buttons down her back until she felt the cool air against her skin. But he didn't stop kissing her, and gradually she felt her whole body coming to life.

He lifted his head for one second—just long enough to slide her gown off her shoulders. She felt the fabric pool at her feet. And then he stepped close to her once more. But instead of kissing her mouth, he bent his head to kiss her shoulder. His fingers tangled in the corset laces she'd tied in front, deftly undoing them, loosening them…and then pulling away the boning and heavy fabric.

When he took her nipple in his mouth through her shift, she tilted her head back. Her breath came shorter and shorter. And yet…

She opened her eyes. He was intent on her, his hands gentle on her skin. But she hadn't wanted to simply give herself to him. She'd wanted to be brave and maybe a little outrageous. And so slowly, she reached out and put her hands on the placket of his trousers. His eyes shut; she could feel the hard length of his erection through the fabric.

"God, Rose."

This was what she needed to do—not just to give herself to him, but to take him in return. Her hands were not so practiced as his had been on her buttons, but he didn't seem to care. He pressed his hips against her hand, urged her as she peeled back his trousers. His smallclothes came next, revealing a long, pale shaft, already swelling under her attentions. She ran a finger over the tip; he gave a little growl.

And then she looked up at him.

"There we are," Rose said, feeling her lips curl into a smile. "Stephen Shaughnessy, Actual Man."

He let out a laugh—but before he could say anything else, before she could lose her nerve—she took him entirely in her hand, caressing him from tip to stem. It was the most amazing thing, the male organ—responsive, moving ever so slightly with her every touch. His breath grew uneven; his shaft pulsed in her hands, growing harder and longer.

"Rose." He set his hand on her shoulder. "Let me have a turn at you, love."

She looked up at him. And then, ever so gently, he pushed her down to the bed. Her heart was beating wildly; she couldn't quite believe she was about to do this.

But then he came over her. He let his weight settle into her, slowly, ever so slowly, until their hips fit together, until her breasts brushed his chest through her last under layer. He kissed her first on the shoulder, then on the chin, and then, tilting her head up, on the lips. That kiss on the lips didn't stop. She let herself sink into it as his body settled against hers. They were hip to hip, separated only by the sheer fabric of her chemise. It was both too much and not enough. Their bodies found a rhythm together, a push and pull like heartbeats, like the tide of gravity between them.

He pulled away from her—only long enough to sweep her chemise up her body, to bare her to the cool air. He took off his shirt, revealing wiry muscles. And then he looked in her eyes. "Four months," he said with a shake of his head. "Truly, we're going to have a four month engagement?"

"It will have to be long enough to forestall all gossip."

"Four months." He made a noise, but he was smiling at her. "Then I'll fetch a French letter and we'll be very careful."

She wasn't sure what to say to that.

He turned from her momentarily, and found something in his dresser. He fitted this to his erection, and then turned to her. "Now it's my turn to prepare you."

He advanced on her. But instead of getting atop her once more, he spread her legs and then very slowly, slid his fingers between them.

"God," he said, "you're beautiful. Beautiful and wet for me. And I can't wait to taste you."

And then he did. He set his mouth to her, and she felt the sure sweep of his tongue. It was the most shockingly intimate thing she'd ever experienced—entirely beyond her imagination—to have him doing this, tasting her, finding that nub there. He slid a finger inside her. Her breath caught. Between his hand and his tongue, she couldn't think, could only experience a sweet pleasure, growing. Her body felt restless. She pushed against him, wanting...

He pulled back ever so slightly. And then, while her body was still desperate for more, he kissed his way up her hips, her navel. His mouth left a warm imprint against her belly, rising up her body rib by rib until he found the rounding edge of her breast.

He took her nipple in his mouth again just as he began to move his finger inside her. Those two points—so deliciously, utterly warm—drove her into a frenzy. She was close to something, so close, and if only he would...

But he didn't. He took his hand away. She almost protested, but he came over her again. This time, he set his erection to her cleft.

"Rose, darling."

She looked up at him.

"I love you," he said.

He slid into her. She'd expected it to be painful and rough, but by the time he entered her, she was already wet and ready for him. There was a pinch—she caught her breath—he stopped...

And she could feel the tip of him inside her, warm and hard, could feel him on top of her, his muscles cording as he held himself back. She reached up tentatively and set her hand on his chest. Very slowly, she drew her fingers down his chest. He made a noise in his throat; his hips flexed, and he slid inside her another inch, and then another, moving slowly until he had filled her completely. Their bodies were joined intimately. She looked up at him...

He smiled, reached down, and brushed her cheek.

"Well," he said. "I had better make sure that you like this. Because four months from now, I'm having you again and again and again."

He moved his hips, pulling out of her and then sliding back—over and over, until that rhythm they'd found before swept them both up. Until her skin seemed to catch fire, and his hands came to her hips. She felt herself come apart around him; he gritted his teeth and then, just as she thought she could take no more, gasped and pounded into her one last time.

They drifted afterward. They'd scarcely slept the night before, and she could not keep her eyes open. She fell asleep to the feel of his fingers against her temples, and the soft murmur of his voice.

"Damn," he said. "Four months."

⌘ ⌘ ⌘

"FOUR MONTHS."

It was six that evening, and Rose's parents—who had journeyed hours through ice and snow to see their first grandchild—sat at the dinner table, frowning at Stephen Shaughnessy.

"Four months," her father repeated. "Is there any reason the engagement must be so short?"

They had already interrogated Stephen on his finances and his family. Her father had muttered when he'd said he was Irish, and frowned when he mentioned that he did some work for a newspaper. Rose had thumped her father, urging him to behave...and when Stephen gave a cheeky answer, had done the same to him. But Stephen had actually comported himself in an almost respectable manner.

If someone didn't say something soon, her parents would have the surprise of their lives when they discovered the things she hadn't told them. She really was going to have to show them one of his columns. If her father discovered it on his own...

"In fact," Stephen said, "I should like the engagement to be shorter."

Right. An excellent way to introduce the topic of his reputation to her parents. Rose managed to hide her wince.

Her father stiffened, glaring at Stephen. But her fiancé—oh, how lovely that word was—simply leaned casually back in his chair, as if he'd not announced to the entire room—to both her parents, watching in wide-eyed shock—that he wanted to take her to bed, and soon.

Which, really, her parents ought to have guessed that from the circumstance of his wanting to marry her, but then parents could sometimes be willfully blind about such things.

"You see," Stephen said piously, "my understanding is that Doctor Wells is expected home any day now. Once he's back, there will be no need for Rose to stay here. And once her sister has recovered herself from the birth... Well, I think Doctor and Mrs. Wells might enjoy having some privacy."

"She'll come home to us in London," her father growled. "Of course she will."

"But then how will she work with Dr. Barnstable?" Stephen asked. He reached out and took her hand under the table. "She enjoys her work with him so, and I would hate to see my Rose deprived of something she liked simply because I was loathe to commit to marriage on a reasonable timeline."

Oh, that was clever.

Her father huffed. "Oh, you're good." He glanced suspiciously at his son-in-law-to-be. "A little too good."

"Oh, no," Stephen said angelically. "I'm afraid not. You'll likely hear about it all too soon. It's the only reason I'm agreeing to four months at all—because if I had insisted on three weeks, the gossip would be too fierce."

Rose's father sighed, but before he could say anything more, the front door opened.

Rose heard stomping feet, a dull thud—and then a man stepped into the back room. His dark skin was more weathered than when last she'd seen him. His hair was cut close to the scalp; a light brush of gray at his temples made him seem all the more austere. He wore a scarlet band on his arm over his uniform.

"Rosie?" He blinked, looking around the room in confusion. "What is going on? Where's Patricia?"

Rose let go of Stephen's hand and sprang to her feet, uttering a little cry of joy. "Isaac! You're back. Oh, you're back. Patricia had the baby—"

"What?"

"And she's well—and he is well—you must come see them now."

"Wait," her father was saying. "We're not done here. I haven't agreed yet."

"Papa," Rose said, "don't let him fool you. He's a rogue and an outrage." She winked at her father. "And once you know him, you'll like him very well. I promise."

Stephen met her gaze, and then, ever so slowly, he smiled. "Ah," he said with a shake of his head. "I love it when you talk sweetly to me."

Epilogue

December, 1882

Dear Man,

    I do not wish to know what the average man wants in a woman; I wish to know what you want in a woman. Tell me, how is a woman like me ever to attract you?
    —Blushing in Bedford

Dear Blushing,

    Over the years of my writing this column, I have received literally thousands of letters asking this question. Until now, I have never answered.
    I don't ask for much in a woman. I like mathematics, astronomy, and women who can multiply nine-digit numbers in their heads. The difficult part was convincing her to like me back.
    You had all better wish her luck. I think she'll need it.
    Sincerely hers,
    Stephen Shaughnessy
    Committed Man

Thank you!

Thanks for reading *Talk Sweetly to Me*. I hope you enjoyed it!

    • Would you like to know when my next book is available? You can sign up for my new release e-mail list at www.courtneymilan.com, follow me on twitter at @courtneymilan, or like my Facebook page at http://facebook.com/courtneymilanauthor.

    • Reviews help other readers find books. I appreciate all reviews, whether positive or negative.

    •*Talk Sweetly to Me* is a companion novella in the Brothers Sinister series. The books in the series are *The Governess Affair*, a prequel novella, *The Duchess War*, *The Heiress Effect*, *The Countess Conspiracy*, *The Suffragette Scandal*, and *Talk Sweetly to Me*. I hope you enjoy them all!

Other Books by Courtney

The Worth Saga
Coming late 2014
click here to find out more

The Brothers Sinister Series
The Governess Affair
The Duchess War
A Kiss for Midwinter
The Heiress Effect
The Countess Conspiracy
The Suffragette Scandal
Talk Sweetly to Me

The Turner Series
Unveiled
Unlocked
Unclaimed
Unraveled

Not in any series
What Happened at Midnight
The Lady Always Wins

The Carhart Series
This Wicked Gift
Proof by Seduction
Trial by Desire

Author's Note

THE IDEA FOR THIS BOOK came from two places. The first was a course in quantum mechanics that I took way back in 2001, one taught by Dr. Jerzy Cioslowski. Dr. Cioslowski was the sort of person who told a million extraneous stories as he taught. One of his stories was of Hartree, one of the early giants of quantum mechanical computations. His main advantage, Cioslowski said, was that his father was a computer: He would calculate all his sums for him, leaving Hartree free to do most of the work.

Once, he told us, the computer was a person. In fact, computers were often women. He said this—leaving half the (female) class sputtering, and then went on blithely.

There isn't much known about the history of female computers. They came into prominence in World War II, when female computers served in the Manhattan project, and helped crack the German's Enigma code. But they existed before that. Very little is said about the computer, either male or female, so I've had to interpolate.

The other source of inspiration for this was a real woman. Her name is Shakuntala Devi, and she was known as the human computer for her ability to calculate complex cube roots in her head in a matter of seconds. Her roots were modest—her father was a circus performer—but not only was she a mathematical genius, she also wrote cookbooks, nonfiction on homosexuality, nonfiction on learning mathematics, and novels (many of these are available as ebooks today). She even ran for office.

In terms of the work Rose was doing, I ended up deleting a lot of astronomy and mathematics from this book as written. (I'm sure you're shocked to hear that.) One of the things I deleted was a reason why she'd be using the law of gravitation to calculate the Great Comet's trajectory. This was actually a huge open problem in astronomy at the time: everyone knew that comets didn't purely obey the laws of gravitation in their trajectory around the sun, and nobody could figure out *why* they didn't. It was a source of some serious disagreement. People came up with all kinds of theories as to the source of the discrepancy. The real answer—asymmetric outgassing of cometary materials as the comet approached the sun, and a few relativistic effects—was not known for many years yet. Rose's goal in her calculations would be to try to fit the theory of gravitation with the other known theories to see which of those theories best approximated reality.

Yes, there was once a lengthy explanation of this in the book. Yes, I deleted it.

As for Patricia's husband, the brief account that Rose gives is also accurate. Africanus Horton, the first black doctor in England, was sponsored by the editor of the *African Times*. Thereafter, several others were sponsored regularly, many of whom married women in England (some white). While we don't have statistics of this by race, by 1882, Britain had probably trained at least as many black doctors as there were dukes. There were also a number of middle-class black families like the one Rose comes from—shopkeepers, lawyers, and the like. I don't pretend there were many of them as a proportion of the population as a whole, but especially in the areas of the country that were near the major ports—Liverpool, London, Manchester and the like—there were known concentrations of people of color. I'm indebted to the book *Black Victorians, Black Victoriana* for their work in peering into the historical record on this point.

Finally, a brief note on the transit of Venus. Just about everything Rose says about the transit of Venus is true. I made one alteration to reality for the purposes of the story. In reality, the snow on December 6th started before the transit did, and so the transit was not visible at all in London. I moved the storm back a few hours, and gave Rose that first glimpse of the phenomenon. I hope you'll forgive that tiny alteration.

Acknowledgments

Some books have a natural story to them, one that takes me almost no effort to write. Others require substantially more work on my part to uncover. This was a book that I thought I understood...until I started writing it and found that the story I'd hoped to tell was not at all the one that showed up on the page. It took me longer to put together than I had hoped.

But I had promised my husband that, for the first time in five years, when we took a vacation, I would not have a pending deadline. (The number of times he has gone out and entertained himself while I struggled with a manuscript back at the hotel room is huge. It's happened in London, Hawaii, Chamonix, New York, Chicago, while visiting his parents, while visiting my parents...) The people who helped me with this book did so under extraordinary deadline pressures: Robin Harders, Keira Soleore, Martin O'Hearn, Martha Trachtenberg, Maria Fairchild, Rawles Lumumba... All of them got this book and turned it around in absolutely record time.

This is the final book in the Brothers Sinister series, and it feels strange to let it go. This series has found me thousands and thousands of new readers, has allowed me to quit my day job. It seems overly dramatic to call it *life-changing*—but what else do you call something that changes your life? To everyone who has enjoyed this series: thank you for changing my life. Thank you for everything.

I hope I can do my next series justice.

8242922R00058

Printed in Great Britain
by Amazon.co.uk, Ltd.,
Marston Gate.